aquasynthesis

splashdown vol. 1

With stories by
Fred Warren, Caprice Hokstad, P. A. Baines,
Adam Graham, R. L. Copple, Travis Perry, Mike Lynch,
Keven Newsome, Kat Heckenbach, Ryan Grabow,
Grace Bridges and Walt Staples

aquasynthesis

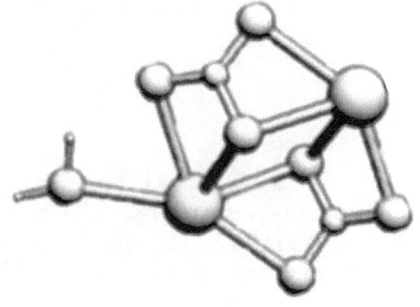

edited by grace bridges
narrated by walt staples

Aquasynthesis
ISBN: 978-1-927154-48-9
Copyright Splashdown Books 2011
Cover Art by DeAnna Newsome, http://newsomecreative.net
All rights reserved

Edited by Grace Bridges
Narrated by Walt Staples

Editor's Assistants:
Diane M. Graham, Kat Heckenbach, Robynn Tolbert, Travis Perry

Narrator's Assistant:
Keven Newsome

Published by Splashdown Books, New Zealand
http://www.splashdownbooks.com

"Facing the Cave" by R.L. Copple—first published in *Mindflights*, February 2008

"Dude" by Kat Heckenbach—first published in *Residential Aliens*, April 2010

"Second Site" by Grace Bridges—first published in *Digital Dragon Magazine*, August 2009

"The Artist" by Kat Heckenbach—first published in *Mindflights*, November 2009, and in *Beyond Centauri*, July 2010.

"A Stretch of Time" by Grace Bridges—first published in *Residential Aliens*, July 2010

"One Smile at a Time" by Fred Warren—first published in *Mindflights*, October 2009

"Faith's Fire" by R.L. Copple—first published in the novel *Reality's Dawn* (Splashdown Books), March 2011; Originally published in *Infinite Realities* as "Unseen Realities" (Double-Edged Publishing, Inc), November 2007.

"The Unjust Judge" by Adam Graham—first published in *Residential Aliens*, April 2011

"Dry Places" by Travis Perry —first published in *Nova Science Fiction Magazine*, 2003

"The Assistant" by Keven Newsome—first published at *The New Authors Fellowship*, February 2011

"Ears" by P.A. Baines—first published at *Where the Map Ends*, December 2010

"Lily's Tale" by Grace Bridges—first published in *OtherSheep* magazine, 2011

"Gravity" by Travis Perry—first published in *Nova Science Fiction Magazine*, 2003

"Your Average Ordinary Alien" by Adam Graham—first published in *Light at the Edge of Darkness* (The Writer's Café Press), 2007

"Weapons of War" by R.L. Copple—first published at *Ray Gun Revival Radio Podcast*, October 2006 (With Honorable Mention)

"A Small Sacrifice" by Mike Lynch—first published in *Digital Dragon Magazine*, August 2009

"Closer to Home" by Keven Newsome—first published in *Digital Dragon Magazine*, August 2010

aqua (n)—water, used in compound names, or substances in water.

synthesis (n)—a joining of elements into a unified entity.

aquasynthesis (n)—a combining of worlds within a pool of water; an anthology of stories from Splashdown authors.

contents

introduction

Grace Bridges

Do you remember diving into the water as a child?

You leap from your perch, a bit scared of the wet world waiting below. The exhilaration of flight. The rush of air. The tingly anticipation of a good soaking.

Then, the splashdown.

You hit the surface. It surprises you, even though you knew it was coming, even though you've done this a hundred times before.

In a second the cool wetness submerges you. You are immersed in the embrace of an alien world. Strange noises fill your ears. You cannot breathe. Peering through the murk, you glimpse a fish, a waterweed, a sandy seafloor, riverbed, or pool tiling. Slanting sunbeams play through the ripples.

You are refreshed and revitalised. Your body propels you back to the world of air and light. You burst out of the water and yell just for the fun of it.

Change of scene, from the familiar to the fantastic. You are an astronaut inside a tiny lifepod. The journey has been long, but finally you are arriving on a new planet. Consider what lies ahead as you approach splashdown time. It's been lonely out there, and you eagerly anticipate meeting other beings again. Feeling your toes sink into dirt, seeing buildings kiss the sky, tasting food that isn't just mush. Even if those beings, that dirt, those buildings and those foods are like nothing you've ever known before.

You have come to a new world. This runs through your head as your capsule hits the alien ocean. Water bubbles up around the window. Gravity sucks you down and down and down. It reminds you of that other picture, jumping from the wharf in childhood—this plunge into the wet, this foreign underwater world. For a moment you wonder if this sea has the same flotation properties as the salty brine of your home.

Then the downwards movement eases and you sense you are ascending. How far down did you go? The gases inside your lifepod now rush you up towards the new atmosphere. What will you find in this new world?

It is with these thoughts of water and discovery that we present Aquasynthesis for your enjoyment. Why Aquasynthesis, and why the H_2O on the cover with its composite parts? Because Splashdown is all about water and all about teamwork. My heartfelt thanks to all the contributors, whether authors, editors, assistants or designers. It is your synthesis that has made this project possible.

Splashdown Books promotes an international team of Christian writers of speculative fiction, their short works synthesised here in a unified story structure. I decided to let each author keep their native spelling, so don't be surprised if you read both American and British variants. These are the things that give our synthesis its flavour, along with the mix of humour and impact, and about every speculative genre you can think of.

And now, dear reader, it is your turn to synthesise with us…and let Walt introduce you to Gizile and Tok, who will guide you from the first page to the last. Dive in with us!

Grace Bridges
Auckland, New Zealand
August 1, 2011

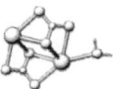

Gizile shivered as she followed the tall, sour-faced man. Raw winter wind blew across the beach and cut through the cloak she clutched about her.

"It's cold," she said. A grunt was her only answer.

She looked at the rolling waves and watched them crawl toward her feet. When they retreated, icy crystals sparkled on the sand.

"Master Tok, for the past six months I've been a quiet student and have learned all you've had to teach. I think I've earned at least one answer. This cold will be the death of us. Why are we here?"

Master Tok paused and gave her a sidelong look. It was a look she knew well, and Gizile lowered her gaze to the sand.

"I'm sorry, Master Tok. I spoke out of turn."

He grunted again, this time in agreement. "You have learned much," he said. "But you have not learned enough." He continued forward.

Gizile sprinted to catch up. "Yes, Master Tok."

They came to a halt at some rocks at the water's edge. Tok pointed at a small tidal pool. "Watch, observe, see and decide. Learn."

She looked up at him. The grayness of her master—gray of hair and eye, gray of complexion, gray of dress, gray of mood—blended almost seamlessly with the gray winter sky.

"What am I supposed to see?" she asked.

He said nothing but continued to point. Gizile tamped down the little flare of indignation his dourness sparked. She moved to a low rock above the pool. The waves lapped over the seaward rim at the end of their run, before they fled back to their home. She bent over the pool, hands on knees, and looked into its depths. A wave flowed in. Crystalline ice erupted over the water like an intricate web. It hardened and turned white. Confused, Gizile stared at the frozen pool.

A picture took shape over its surface. A picture that moved, as if it were a window to another world. Gizile held her breath. And watched.

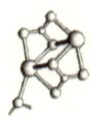

Facing the cave

R. L. Copple

"And though countless have tried," the bard said to the tavern audience, "the dragon that never dies continues to devour all who come to its cave."

Galak clapped with those in the tavern but noticed Sir Humblart, his teacher and friend, staring as if into another world. When Galak saw Sir Humblart's jaw set, he knew the story had stirred a desire in his master. Galak took another gulp from his stein in hopes of numbing the rising fear.

Sir Humblart rose from his seat. "Come, Squire. We have a dragon to slay."

The bard laughed. "Didn't you hear me? This dragon is death itself. No man can defeat death."

Sir Humblart smiled and his eyes lit as they always did when he said something of importance. "Correct. No man can, if none attempts it."

"Attempt away! The dragon is always hungry." Laughter erupted from the patrons.

Sir Humblart nodded. "And if I return from death, then what?"

The bard stumbled over words then blurted out, "I'll believe that when I see it!" More guffaws arose.

Sir Humblart downed the last of his ale and motioned for Galak to follow.

After grabbing supplies, Sir Humblart led Galak through the forest toward the undefeated foe.

"Sir, I have your sword," Galak said.

Sir Humblart didn't turn his head. "I'll have no cause for such weapons. Keep hold of it. You will need it."

Their feet crunched the dirt and dried leaves on the forest floor as they pushed toward—what? His death? Galak watched the armor-clad knight marching resolutely to face the monster that had sent so many to Hell's gates. No hint of fear twitched across his face. No evidence of second thoughts surfaced in those coal-black, unblinking eyes.

In due time, they entered the clearing where the dragon's cave bore into the mountain. Strewn across the knoll lay scorched armor and rusted swords. Bones rested thick across the grass, piled by the cave opening. Many lives had been spent attempting to destroy the dragon. Legend had it that the souls of all those killed here wandered without rest, trapped by the dragon.

A roar erupted from beneath the earth, and the ground shook. Smoke belched from the entrance as if dust long undisturbed exploded from its cloisters. Mournful cries underlaid the horrific noise; Galak wanted to cry with them.

Galak fled behind a tree as he watched the beast burst from the cave and land a few feet from Sir Humblart. A mélange of greens and browns shimmered in the sunlight on its hide. The slender body tapered to a tail, which whipped to and fro. The other end held aloft a neck three times as long as any man's body. At the end of the neck, a broad head examined Sir Humblart with fiery eyes, and a forked tongue lashed the air.

"Sir, flee before it's too late!" Galak yelled out.

Sir Humblart turned to Galak. "To free them, I must die." He faced the dragon, his feet together, lifted his arms as if to fly, and cast his head forward.

Now Galak knew his master had lost his mind. Perhaps the villagers brewed a stouter ale than they had realized. He cowered behind the tree as a deafening roar caused him to cover his ears in pain. But he couldn't remove his gaze from Sir Humblart.

The beast's head dove, and its open mouth scooped in Sir Humblart. Its head flung back. Galak watched as a bulge slid down the dragon's neck. Apparently satisfied with its meal, the dragon lumbered to the cave.

Galak's stomach twisted, and bile rose up his throat. Hot tears rolled down his cheeks. Then he remembered: he still had the sword. He could yet save his master and friend. An attempt would likely end in death, but love demanded no less. He steeled himself, unsheathed the weapon, drew himself to his feet, and prepared to charge.

The dragon halted before reaching the cave. A mournful cry shattered the air, and the dragon thrashed about, as if attempting to throw an invisible rider. It spun and writhed until another shriek filled Galak's ears. He fell to his knees; the sword dropped to the ground.

The dragon teetered and fell over onto its side with a ground-shaking crash. Galak peered at it, but the dragon no longer moved.

The ground rumbled until a blast of air exploded from the cave and twirled into a vortex. Galak swore he heard joyous singing within the gale. The bones around him rattled before the swirling wind sucked them into its grip, and they flew beyond the mountain and into the sky.

The pull of the music and push of the wind encouraged Galak. He crept toward the beast, eyeing it through wind-whipped hair, ready to flee, but it did not move. Not until Galak came close enough did he see a bulge pushing against the skin.

He gasped and stumbled in haste to retrieve the sword. He raced back to the carcass and swung the sword two-handed upon the base of the neck. Green blood spewed forth, and with it the dragon's body vomited out Sir Humblart, covered in chunky, pea-green slime.

In his acid-seared hand, Sir Humblart held a heart the size of a grown man's head. He arose and cast a bright gaze upon Galak.

"No man can escape death. It can only be defeated from within. And now, I have destroyed it." Sir Humblart cast the heart into the cave.

Galak's pulse quickened as Sir Humblart's eyes pierced through him. The master turned and proceeded down the path to the village.

Galak followed, as he had always done—but now, through death to life.

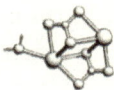

"What is this? I don't understand. Dragons? Is this a portal to another world? Are we safe? How did you…"

Tok laughed, a low rumble Gizile had never heard from him before.

Gizile's mouth opened in shock. "You laugh at my questions, Master?"

"You have much to learn, young one. One thing you must learn is to laugh. And to trust. Would I show you something that could be of harm to you?"

Shame filled her. He had always protected her and taught her with wisdom. But she needed to *know*. "Was what I saw true? Was it just a story? How did you show me this? What do I learn from—"

"Enough!"

Gizile felt her face redden despite the frigid air. She hung her head.

"Too many questions!" he growled. "Watch and learn."

Gizile shivered and turned back to the pool. A wave. An explosion of ice over the surface. And a new picture formed. A young man…with pointed ears.

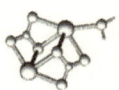

dude

Kat Heckenbach

"It looks like snot."

"What's your point, Frankie?"

If Frankie had been anything less than a computer language *genius* I wouldn't allow him in my classroom, much less hire him as a lab assistant.

"Well, dude…"

I lifted my gaze from the microscope in front of me and glared at him.

"Uh, sorry, Dr. Simeon, ma'am. I was gonna say, I knew it wouldn't look like that twisted ladder thingy…"

"The double helix, Frankie."

Nowhere in any of Tolkien's works had I read anything about Elves like Frankie. He was just over six feet tall and no more than a hundred and sixty pounds, with white-tipped, spiked hair that mimicked the points of his ears. His usual outfit included a striped t-shirt and parachute pants right out of the eighties. His parents had moved to America in 1987, and clung to all the wrong elements of the culture. The result—an Elven brain wasted on video games and skateboarding. Still, he could write programs that were capable of, well, pretty much anything.

"Yeah, double helix. Sounds like a cool name for a rock band." He snorted at his own joke and wiped his nose on his shirt. The extracted DNA hanging from the wire loop in his hand jiggled. He was right. It did look like snot.

I looked at the clock, the sole decoration on the walls of my second-floor lab. I didn't bother with anything other than essentials. Like I could afford more on this budget. *Sigh.* Nearly eleven. How had it gotten so late?

Frankie stood there staring blankly at the slimy string of unraveled chromosomal material. I was beginning to wonder why I bothered teaching him to help me with this part.

"So, du—I mean, Dr. S, you're really gonna chop this up and send it to someplace that can tell you all those little letters?"

"Nucleotides, Frankie. And as you so crudely put it, we will 'chop up' DNA, yes, but not *that* particular piece."—I'd kill to have the equipment to sequence DNA myself, but that takes money this little university doesn't have—"I just want you to have an idea of what I'm doing here. So you understand your part in this."

"Frankie Davis, über-geek extraordinaire. At your service, ma'am." He bowed with a flourish, the motion offering the tiniest glimpse into the kind of Elf he might have been if he'd been raised in his homeland. The DNA strand slipped off the loop onto the floor. "Uh, sorry, Dr.S."

I rubbed my temple, and that spot in my back tightened. Everything in my core believed this Earth had been created by a higher power, an Intelligent Designer. God. But looking at Frankie, with his crooked, spaced-out expression, I could kind of see the whole human-ape connection. Or, at least, the elf-ape connection. Either way, it was disheartening.

Frankie grinned, and suddenly that light in his eyes clicked on, the one that had made me hire him. It seemed to only appear when he sat in front of his computer or thought about the program he was writing for me.

"I've been workin' like a fiend, Dr. S. The code's flowin' like a river." He waved his hands in front of his waist like a hula dancer, and then straightened back up with a look of pride. "My best work yet. Totally righteous."

"I appreciate it, Frankie. I know it's a lot of work, and this semester is really tough for you."

Frankie was actually a biology major. A computer-programming savant, and he wanted to "swim with the dolphins." Go figure.

"No prob. It's fun." His smile dropped a notch and his forehead furrowed. His words came out with a depth I'd never heard in his speech before. "I'm really close to finishing, Dr. S, but…I wish you'd tell me exactly what the program is looking for."

I couldn't do that before, for fear it would influence him. I had merely given him certain parameters on which to base his program. The experiment couldn't be impacted by my beliefs. It had to be impartial.

My beliefs didn't affect the research I did for the university, of course. Beyond the origin of life, science is science. Breeding fruit flies and splicing genes into *salmonella* doesn't rock any boats. But my personal research, that's a different story.

"You're really almost done writing the program?" I asked.

My heart felt like it might thud to a stop. I could be crossing a line here, one I wouldn't be able to retrace. But, maybe it was time. Frankie had already discovered the Bible in my desk drawer. He didn't comment when he found it, and I didn't offer an explanation.

"What I tell you at this point will have no bearing on your program— you're sure?" I sat back in my chair and studied his face. He nodded and gazed at me with anticipation. I decided to go for it.

"Well, Frankie, the Bible tells us that God is the Creator of the universe, and we see His building blocks everywhere. He's also called the *Author* of life. He *wrote* our DNA. He must have signed His work somewhere."

His eyes twinkled as he drew out his words in hushed tones. "Dude...I mean, Dr. S..."—his mouth slipped into a smile—"that is, like...the most righteous thing I've ever heard."

I couldn't stop my cheeks from pulling back. Years of discrimination by university staff melted away at that moment. I wanted to hug the spiky-haired kid sitting across the table from me. Instead, I straightened the collar of my lab coat.

"Well, then, Frankie. I mean, *dude.* Let's get to work."

As a wave washed in, shattering the ice and dragging it out to sea, Gizile became self-conscious and reached up to feel the tip of her own ear. She had so many questions, now, but she dare not ask. Looking up at her master again, she found him staring at her.

"This one was kin to the last, did you see it, child?"

"I…no," she stammered. "They seemed nothing alike."

"Yet they both had strange creatures, a quest, and something else."

"W…what was that, Master?"

"Slime," he said with a twinkle in his eye that seemed completely unlike the master she thought she had known for six long months. "Now look!" he commanded, his gray manner suddenly returning.

She bit her lip and turned back to the water. It had already frozen again. And on the surface, a man in a red suit reached into a bag.

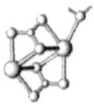

old saint nick

Travis Perry

Old Saint Nick reached into the bag of toys around the corner of the hallway at the far left side of the ninety-eighth floor of the skyscraper. He drew out what looked like a miniature chimney. Hefting it onto his shoulder, he swung back around the corner and fired it.

With a flash, a chimney-hole shaped box flew from the end. Silver ribbons flapped in curls around bright, blue wrapping until the projectile smashed into an eight-legged alien down the hall.

Boom!

Green blood and yellow slime decked the halls. The creature screeched and squirmed for less time than it took Santa to slide down a chimney. Then, silent night.

More aliens, further down the hall, leapt over the body of their fallen comrade and rushed the Jolly Old Elf, hoping, it seemed, to overwhelm him with sheer numbers. Saint Nick didn't miss a beat, popping off each one in turn with a gift from his Chimney Bazooka.

Suddenly, a thunk shook the ground behind Saint Nick. He whirled and saw an enormous alien, maw gaping. He froze. Before he could say, "MERRY CHRISTMAS," a tip of a sword appeared through the alien's belly. The sword tip moved sideways in two quick flicks, bisecting the monster.

The top half of the alien quivered and fell to the floor, revealing

Santa's savior—Rimbo the black elf. He wiped the green blood off his vorpal blade.

"Dude! You saved my life, man. You rock!" Santa's voice squeaked.

"This game is OK," said the elf, "but I'd rather be playing *Grand Car Theft VR*. That's got real blood. And hookers." The elf waggled his eyebrows.

"Dude! It's Christmas Eve! Show some freaking holiday spirit!"

"Respect. So where do we go now?"

"I dunno, man. You're a way better Rimbo than the computer. It always gets killed before this, so I've never made it this far before. I think we got just one more hallway." The virtual red-suited Saint pointed toward the right.

"OK. You lead the way and I'll cover your jolly fat butt!"

"Man, don't talk about Santa's rear end that way. It's just wrong."

"Yeah, what*ever*, dude."

They hunkered forward into the hall. Saint Nick pivoted back and forth, pointing the chimney into the open doorways that lined each side of the hallway, attempting stealth in spite of his immense girth and bright-red "camouflage." Rimbo walked backwards, behind Santa, his vorpal blade at the ready, his black tights and suit making him significantly less visible than his companion.

"Hey! You know, we're like, basically the same as Batman and Robin," said Rimbo, "except for them, the big fat guy wears a dark suit, while the little guy wears red."

"Shhhh! Listen." Both stopped walking and Santa cocked an eye at the ceiling. "Do you hear that?"

Just then the ceiling tiles broke apart and nasty-yellow-slimy-chomping-teeth aliens tumbled down, filling the hallway before and behind them. They were surrounded.

"HO!" shouted Santa, half-goofy, half-serious, chimney belching flames as he fired.

"HO, HO, dude!" laughed Rimbo, his blade severing those aliens foolish enough to approach him, as easy as a hot knife through butter.

Some of the aliens made leaps worthy of a basketball virtual reality slam-dunk contest. Still, Santa's chimney blew them back. Things were dicier on the other side, where the monsters could easily advance to biting distance, despite the dark elf's twirling blade.

Rimbo ducked and sliced and thrust with skill, nimbly avoiding even a tooth mark. But the severed body parts of those leaping at him from on high continued their forward momentum after he slashed and ducked, which caused them to slam into Santa's back.

"Hey, man! I'm taking damage! Whassup with that?"

"You can feel that?"

"No, man, like, duh! We're only wired for sight and sound. It's my health meter, its going down, dude!"

"Sorry, man! I'm busy!"

The colored bar showed Saint Nick's health, visible only from the inside of his virtual reality goggles, ticking down until it glowed red. But Santa stood his ground until the hallway cleared. Surrounded by severed and burned alien body parts, splattered with yellow and green goo, he turned to Rimbo.

"Dude! We cleared the level! Now we have to face the boss, up on the 99th floor. Then we'll, you know, be done with Downtown World!"

"Cool! So let's get moving." They took the elevator up.

The elevator doors opened. Santa and the dark elf stepped out into a cavernous room, with glass ceiling and walls, suitable for a truly gigantic monster. Crystalline chandeliers provided only a dim overhead glow. They could see the sparkling nighttime lights of the metropolis out the windows, through the lightly falling snow. In the center of the room, a water fountain, of the sort you'd see in a city park, sprayed plumes of white high into the air.

"Santa Dude, the ceiling must be, like, fifty or sixty feet high."

"Yeah. And I think this room takes up the whole floor."

"So, where's the boss?"

"I dunno. Hey, look! I think I see something on the other side of the fountain!" Through the white plumes of spraying water, at the opposite rim of the fountain, was a shape that might have been a man.

Rimbo pointed to himself then gestured a circling motion to the right. He pointed next at Santa, and then indicated a circling motion to the left. Santa nodded.

They eased their way around the four-foot fountain wall, each moving in the opposite direction, each peering through the obscuring waters, looking for any sign of movement from the figure on the other side.

There was none.

Then they were there, on either side of an old man. Tall and thin, with a long white beard, long white robe, and olive-hued skin. He sat on the edge of the fountain wall. He turned his head, focusing his dark brown eyes first on Rimbo, then Santa.

"Whassup?" said the old man.

He hopped off the wall with youthful agility and stepped toward Santa, who put the open end of the chimney up to the old man's chest. The man in white stopped moving.

"Kill him!" shouted Rimbo. "Kill him!"

"Something isn't right here," said Santa, confused. "Don't move, old man, or I'll blast you!"

"Blast him now!" yelled Rimbo. When the red-suited figure didn't immediately respond, the dark elf leapt forward, his sword outstretched, to run the old man through.

Calmly, without even looking, the man fast-stepped to the side and reached out, grabbing the elf by the wrist of his sword hand. He held the sword away from himself and looked Rimbo in the eye.

"Look, man, I just want to talk to you guys a minute."

Rimbo's eyes widened. "I can FEEL your hand on my wrist."

The old man let go of him. He glanced over to Santa, then looked back at Rimbo. "First, let's settle who I'm not. I'm not the boss of this level. You won't ever see me here again. But who we can call the 'Boss of Bosses' gave me a few minutes to speak with you dudes. He's even granted me the ability to, *like*, speak your language."

"Like," said Santa, "what do you mean? You don't, like, speak English or something? Where are you from? What are you doing hacking into my game?"

"I'm from a town called Myra, in Lycia, in what today is called Turkey. Not the turkey you eat, dudes. Back then we weren't Turks. I grew up speaking Greek. Oh, hey, sorry for not saying so sooner—my name is Nicholas, though you probably know me better as 'Saint Nick'." He held his hand out to his left side, to shake Santa's hand.

Santa kept the chimney leveled at the man in white. "Dude, I don't know how you got in here. This game is supposed to be totally secure. You'd better get out. *Now!*"

"What a minute! Cody, this is, you know, the real Saint Nicholas here! I mean, whoa! Do you live at the North Pole and everything?"

"Erik, this guy's not the real anything! He's just some jerk that hacked into my system!"

"Are you playing online right now?" asked the old man.

"NO."

"Then how could I hack into the game?"

Cody didn't have an answer for that.

The old man still reached out toward him. "Won't you shake my hand, dude?"

"No, I won't." But he did lower the chimney.

The man dropped his hand to his side and turned back to the elf, "Dude, you must be kidding about the North Pole, right? It's, like, in the middle of the Arctic Ocean."

"Really?"

"Word. Hey, and I don't really 'live' anywhere. I died a long time ago."

"Now he's telling us he's, like, a ghost." Cody snorted.

"No, not a ghost—a vision. Hey, sorry, dudes, I don't have time for this. I only got, you know, a minute left and I need to talk, OK?"

They said nothing in reply, but listened, faces turned towards him.

"I hate what people have done with this 'Santa Claus' thing, you know? It's made Christmas so it's about me. I mean, I did give presents to people, but not just on Christmas, and not just to kids. But that's not all I did. I was a bishop, you know, a preacher, a church leader guy. And I never had elves or reindeer or a red suit or hopped down chimneys or anything like that. And I sure never wasted a bunch of aliens. And dudes, I was never, ever fat." He eyed Cody's virtual midsection. "I wasn't even chubby."

"You know why I gave presents?" At first, the question seemed like the kind you ask without expecting an answer. But he stared at them, waiting for a response.

Finally the elf said, "No, why?"

"Because Jesus helped people, by healing them. And his disciples had a moneybag, so they gave away money to people who, you know, really needed help. That's why I gave presents, because *Jesus* did. And isn't Jesus what Christmas is supposed to be about? And giving instead of getting? Kindness instead of cruelty? Right?"

They had no answer for him. The elf's eyes drifted downward.

Old Saint Nick reached behind him and did a short hop to seat himself once more on the wall. "Anyway, dudes, Merry Christmas to you."

With that he lifted his feet, swung around, and scooted off the wall into the fountain. He immediately sank down out of view.

Erik and Cody moved forward and looked over the wall. In the fountain, there was no sign that Saint Nicholas had ever been there.

"That's it! I'm outta this game!" Cody/Santa reached up to his face, pulled off the Virtual Reality helmet, and...

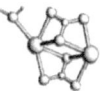

He was back in his room. Erik pulled his VR helmet off too, and, for a brief moment, each looked into his friend's eyes, not recognizing the teenage face in front of him.

"This thing is defective," said Cody as he popped the *Santa Claus Saves the Universe* disk out of the Playcube VR. "I'm gonna get my money back."

"I dunno, man. Did you hear what he said? He was, like, a vision."

"No, man. He was bad programming."

"Dude, I *felt* his hand on my wrist."

"No, man. You imagined it. I almost fell for it, too. But, dude, this is just some programmer's idea of a joke. That's all."

"But dude, I felt him," Erik muttered. "Do you s'pose he was right about Christmas?"

"Dude, you aren't thinking straight. It's late. Let's go to bed."

Erik paused a moment, a thoughtful look on his face. "Sure, man. Hey, Merry Christmas to you."

"Yeah, what*ever*, dude."

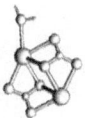

"Master," Gizile said as she turned. His stony stare almost made her abandon her question. But she pressed anyway. "Who were the men in the vision…or game…?"

"You know them by other names, child. Is that all you saw?"

"No, Master. I also saw this shared a word with the one before…what does 'dood' mean?"

Master Tok's lips quirked into something approaching a smile, but he did not answer. She could hear the crackle of the ice setting, so she turned back. A man stared up at her. Gizile's heart almost froze like the water below. After a quiet moment, she waved her hand in front of the man, but he did not see her. It was as if she were looking through the back side of a mirror, and he trapped on the reflective side.

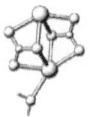

bob

P. A. Baines

Amazing how much blood a nick so small can produce.

My reflection stares back at me from the bathroom mirror. Dark bags under blood-shot eyes. Last night was my first decent sleep since I can't remember when. I used to have no problem sleeping but these days I have too much on my mind. Work has become one big bag of deadlines.

My hair has been given the lying-on-my-head treatment and I look as if I have spent the evening at the business end of a wind-tunnel. What little is left of my hair seems to be rioting over the living conditions.

The razor is getting blunt. A blade a few days old is best—not *too* sharp. Craig at work keeps his blades in a cardboard pyramid under his bed. As long as the dimensions are the same as the Great Pyramid of Cheops, and pointing in the right direction. Swears it keeps them in perfect condition. I make a mental note to buy new ones as the spot of red pushes through the streaks of foam.

The tap in the basin is dripping and I make a mental note to have a look. Same mental note as every day for the past two weeks. My mental notes are getting out of hand. I make a mental note to organize my mental notes.

Water is wet.
Water falls from the sky.
We cry water.
Does the sky cry?

I pull a comb through my hair and select a shirt with fewer creases than the others. The ties all look the same so I choose the one nearest. Yellow blotches mixed with green splashes, blue globs, red streaks, and some colours I can't be bothered to identify. The result is chaotic but pleasing and possibly still in fashion.

I draw the tie over, through, round and down. It tightens against my windpipe. Who decided that a strip of cloth hanging from the neck looks good? Do I look more professional because of something that appears as if it has been subjected to a kindergarten painting lesson?

I slide into my jacket and wriggle until it sits comfortably.

Yes, very professional.

I wonder what Bob would think.

We wear clothes to cover our bodies.
Clothes keep us warm and dry.
The sun keeps us warm and dry.
Can we wear the sun?

The train is late, which does not surprise me. I check my watch. A graduation present from my parents. The second hand glides smoothly across the face. The station clock shows no seconds. Only minutes and hours count in a train station. Seconds are irrelevant when it comes to the mass transportation of people. Why does my watch regard seconds as important? I can't remember ever using the second hand—except to make sure the watch is still working.

Someone speaking with a mouthful of crackers into a fan announces the late arrival of the train. I make out 'train', 'late', 'platform', and possibly 'splib'.

The crowd gathers around me and moves as one organism towards the edge of the platform. I feel uneasy being so close to the front. What if the people at the back don't stop pushing? Would the train be able to stop in time?

In the distance I hear the rumble of metal on metal.

Trains carry people.
People catch trains.
People catch colds.
Do colds carry people?

I find a window seat and gaze out. People are still boarding. Like cattle they amble obediently towards the doors. Personal space sucked in like a beer gut passing through a nightclub. Heads nod to i-pods. Fingers tap messages to unseen soulmates. Cell phones cry out like hatchlings demanding to be fed. Broadsheets crouch, waiting.

Once on board, personal offices open up. Laptop wings unfold, ready to fly the digital sky. Cell phones are fed with loud attention from doting parents. Newspapers pounce and stretch.

Each in his or her own world. So many worlds. Such a small space.

Eyes see the world.
Eyes open and close.
Windows open and close.
Can windows see the world?

I recognize many faces.

My eyes meet those of another and eyebrows are raised in silent greeting. New guy. Whatshisname from Testing. On the edge of my tongue. What *is* his name?

I've been trying a new technique recently. Take the first name and last names of two famous people and imagine them standing on either side of the person you want to remember.

Tina Gibson? No. Silly.

Mel Turner? No no.

George Connery? No no no.

George Turner! Yes, it works. I can clearly see George Clooney and Tina Turner standing either side of geeky George. He smiles his vague smile, peering self-consciously over his glasses before returning to his laptop.

Geeky George Turner from the Testing team. He joined after I left for more interesting pastures. I used to write the tests. Now I run them and analyze the results. I think I was quite good at testing, because I understand how computers work.

People use computers.
Computers run programs.
People run to keep fit.
Are computers trying to keep fit?

Behind Geeky George I see the side of Craig's face. He looks my way and leans over a little so that I can see him squint and pull a tongue at the back of Geeky George's head.

I snicker in spite of myself and look away. The middle-aged woman sitting opposite gives me a cold glare.

Craig is one of the smartest people I know, but naughty. He loves his practical jokes, especially on middle managers who never know how to respond. His favourite is sending spoof emails inviting people for coffee and cake at some poor unsuspecting individual's office.

I keep telling him he'll get into trouble, but he just shrugs and gets a glint in his eye.

I suspect Bob will be given a wicked sense of humour if Craig has anything to do with it. Bob's first act will be to send out an email announcing a manager's sexual-realignment and asking everyone to call him Agnes in future.

People have a sense of humour.
Jokes make people laugh.
Hyenas laugh.
Do hyenas have a sense of humour?

The journey is slow. Progress is tedious. Storm damage on the line. Buildings stroll casually by.

The woman opposite me (Ms. Icy Glare) has picked up her broadsheet and I read the headlines. A hundred people killed by a truck bomb in some city in the Middle East. Further down the page, the search for a missing girl goes on after six weeks. Who was it who said: one death is a tragedy, two deaths a statistic?

The train picks up speed and I watch the houses go by faster and faster until the faces behind the windows become an anonymous blur. I wonder if they wonder about the people on the train. If a bomb exploded in my carriage and I died, would they spare me more than a glance at a headline?

Clocks have working parts.
People have working parts that keep us alive.
When our working parts stop moving we die.
When the working parts in clocks stop moving, do they die?

The train pulls into the station and there is a rush for the doors. Prospects to improve. Resumes to build. The second hand on my watch moves past the six. I hang back with my bag of deadlines. Craig is waiting as well. Bob will have to wait for his sense of humour.

I watch the crowd press into itself. So much anxiety in such a small place.

And why?

What drives us to do anything? What makes what are essentially bags of meat and bones in skirts and suits get up in the morning and do whatever it is we do?

At school my science teacher told us that you could buy all the ingredients for a human for about the same price as a fillet steak. That throw-away remark cost me many nights' sleep as I pondered my own existence.

Was I nothing more than an extra rare steak?

Rene Descartes tried to find a starting point for his philosophies by asking what exactly it was he could know about himself for sure. He didn't trust his senses and decided that it was only his ability to think that was proof of his existence.

An extra rare steak that can think? And not just think, but think about thinking, about thinking…

The door is almost clear. Craig is behind Geeky George again, this time mimicking his slightly lopsided shuffle. He throws me a cheeky grin as they step out onto the platform. I hold back, happy with my own thoughts. About life, the universe, and Bob.

Humans exist.
Computers exist.

Humans can think about thinking.
I do not understand...

The office is a block away and I stroll. Rush hour is chasing its last few victims. The sun peeks at me between two skyscrapers and I bask in a moment of warmth.

I offer my badge to the security guard and he barters me a bored nod.

I stand with two others watching the lift numbers jostling each other for position. I know the faces but not the names. We race upwards in awkward silence, offering subdued greetings at each stop.

My floor is already busy with changing the world. People stare closely into computer screens. Managers walk and talk. Messengers dodge and weave.

I find my desk and log in. A post-it note on my screen says: "nice tie". I see Craig grinning at me from the coffee machine.

I wave my order. Cappuccino, with sugar please waiter.

I check my emails. The data loading job ran all the way through last night. No problems. No hiccups. Enough information to fill a few libraries. Enough to keep every project in the building busy.

But ours is only a small team dealing with basic logic skills. The important work is going on upstairs. Down here we do the baby stuff. The learning-how-to-say-Mama stuff.

"So," Craig says, wheeling his chair across to my desk. "We ready to wake Bob?"

I load the program. The new improved program. A major upgrade from the last version.

A cursor blinks, waiting for me to type.

I open a slim folder containing a single sheet of paper. A list of trigger words and logic questions prepared by Geeky George and his team.

I tap out the first word: "Square."

Bob responds.

`A geometric shape. Four sides of equal length. Four angles of equal size. An area within a building. A nerd.`

I type another word: "River."

`A narrow flowing body of water, moving from a higher elevation to a lower elevation. A final card dealt in` poker. A vertical flow of spaces in a body of text.

I type: "Brother."

`A male sibling. A monk. An African American male.`

I glance at Craig. Now for something a little harder.
"Love."

`An emotion rising from strong affection for another being. A scoring system in tennis. A county in Oklahoma.`

"Happiness."

`An emotion denoted by feelings of pleasure and well-being. A rock band from Finland.`

Craig raises an eyebrow.
"Wealth."

`Well-being. The possession of many items or characteristics of value. An abundance.`

Good. He seems to able to cope with abstract concepts.
I ask: "What is the time?"

`Eight twenty-three.`

"How early is it?"

`It is mid-morning. It is early in the working day. It is earlier than nine o'clock.`

"How long is a piece of string"?
Craig points to the processing meter. This measures how much work the computer is doing. It peaks into the red for a moment.

`That question does not make sense.`

Good. "How high is up?"
The meter stabs into the red.

`That question does not make sense.`

I chuckle. "If all coal is black and all crows are black, are all crows coal?"
The meter hits the red and stays there for a few moments. One or two people look up from their computers.

No. This is a logic error.

"Give more detail on your last statement."

If two objects share one characteristic, this does not mean they are the same object.

Excellent. Craig nods his approval.

I am at the end of the list. No more questions. I look at Craig, who seems to know what I'm thinking.

How about something really tough?

I pause, then type. "Who are you?"

Nothing happens. The screen is blank. For a moment it looks as if the program has frozen, or worse, crashed. Suddenly the meter hits the red and stays there.

I am me. I am myself. I am who I am. I think therefore I am. I am Bob...

There are shouts from around the office. People look up from their stations like meerkats trying to locate a yet-unidentified threat. "Who's using all the processing power?" a manager demands.

I feel the heat rise into my face. The tie becomes a noose around my neck.

Craig sinks lower into his chair. *Oh no. What have we done?*

"The project upstairs! Dammit! Get me operations!"

Managers move from desk to desk looking panic-stricken. The meerkats search frantically...

I am an entity. I am an object. I am real. I exist. I am alive...

The manager shouts—screams—into the telephone. Just cut it! I don't care! Shut the program down, dammit!

He looks up at me.

I look from him to my screen then back again. I raise my hand. No, wait.

I am...

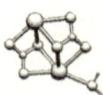

Gizile cocked her head in thought and looked unseeing at the horizon. "Worlds both real and unreal," she murmured. "Life springing out of a machine." Perhaps life was more than she imagined. Perhaps *she* was more than she gave herself credit for.

"Focus."

Master Tok's solitary word cut through her contemplation. She gritted her teeth, feeling as if she had been robbed of an epiphany that was just beyond reach. She looked down at the pool in time to see the ice form yet again. A steely-eyed woman, a tall man, and a strange horseless coach. Gizille leaned forward on her elbows.

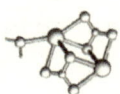

when the game became too real

Ryan Grabow

An excerpt from the novel *Caffeine*

Virtual reality becomes less virtual every day.

By the end of the twenty-second century, today's internet has become a universe unto itself: a place where the imagination of mankind is unleashed, where dreams are indistinguishable from reality. Brandon only wants the same as everyone else...to get away from his life for a few days. He's played these Dynamic Reality games hundreds of times before.

When the AIs start acting strangely and his war-game begins tearing itself apart, Brandon realizes he is trapped in an environment he can't control; then, finding a way back to a real-world that wasn't so real, he questions whether he ever made it back at all.

Reality and fantasy have blurred. Brandon has been shut away from everything and everyone he knows. He demands answers, and finally he encounters the woman who had trapped him in the game, someone who is at home in the virtual world, someone who doesn't seem quite human.

The rain curtain dissolved and I heard the sound of a car behind me. I stood frozen as the amai quietly walked past me.

"If that is the only course of action you will take," she said in a flatter tone, "then that too is opened to you."

I slowly turned and saw her holding the open door of a black limousine. The music from the bar behind me became louder. Friendly voices shouted my name and invited me into my captor's more gentle, intended, method; but the door ahead of me held answers. I knew in my heart that the difficult path was the one I had to follow, even as everything in the place directed me away. Even the amai's perky voice had become plain and unsympathetic.

"Now choose."

I sat uneasily in the back of the limo, the only company being several monitors set to various cameras and broadcast networks. The door closed and the hologram vanished. The car started moving.

"Hey! Where are we—"

The woman appeared in the seat across from me, staring silently into me with hard green eyes, sitting unnaturally straight and giving off the body language of a statue.

"What do you require?"

"I, uh…" I blinked and remembered to breathe.

"Is aimless wandering all you do, Mr. Dauphin?"

"Yeah. Uh…" I took another breath and summoned my energy, finding anger. "Yeah! When I can't reach my family or friends! When I've been kidnapped and held in DR! Yeah, I guess so!"

A glass of wine appeared in my hand.

"A '62 Merlot. Good year. Please tell me what I can do to make up for your trouble."

I let the glass fall. "Let me go and maybe I won't press charges!"

The woman continued to stare unsympathetically. From her sea of apparent indifference, something rose up, barely detectable, hinting at frustration. Though the tone of her words remained flat, the pauses between them became shorter. "I've tried to follow, fool, guide, intimidate then impress you. What other kind of persuasion do I need to give?"

"Persuasion for what?"

She hesitated. "Call it research, for which you are an involuntary subject."

I held out my hand in mock introduction. "I'm sorry, we still haven't been properly introduced. I'm Brandon and y—"

"Brandon Sinden Dauphin of Los Angeles, California; born to Paul and Rachel Dauphin in Nampa, Idaho on the date September 12, 2154, as the youngest of two sons and one daughter. Registered to move to Los Angeles County on date September 15, 2177. Present address: 3400A He—"

"How did you learn so much about me? I've never even seen you before!"

"That isn't relevant."

"You were the one who caused those problems, right? Who caused my Korea simulation to blow itself up? Who caused... whatever that was at the... at the library?"

I detected frustration again and remembered the danger I was in, wondering if the hacker really was the type to kill someone, or if I'd even be her first victim. I realized that her behavior was just as the world outside had been, with everything a little off, cutting along the line between reality and fabrication. I found that I couldn't read her at all, not because there was nothing to be read, but because I couldn't understand what I saw.

Who am I up against? Have I done something to her? Is she unstable? Why is she so interested in me? Why won't she just come out and say it?

"Your Korea program did what it was designed to," she stated, "though I did not understand its appeal."

"And when I got dizzy and almost descended?" I asked, remembering that someone had accessed my ascension booth earlier. "Was that you, too?"

"The construct suffered a break in consistency and your readings indicated a medical emergency. You were not experiencing one, and you are okay now."

"So after this concern for my life, you threaten to kill me?"

"In exchange for your cooperation, I will consider letting you live."

"You talk about death so casually," I said. "I have a..."

Family? Friends? Fiancée? What *do* I have?

I groaned loudly to chase away the tears, wondering if I could even try to make a case to save my life, or if anyone would listen to it.

"I don't want to die," I said powerlessly.

"Is it so much of an offense?" she replied. "Death is part of life, thousands have died in the moment we've been talking; thousands more have been born to replace them. You are only one life."

"*My* life means something to *me*. Couldn't you have picked someone else?"

"And if I had, wouldn't that person ask the same question?"

"I still don't know who I'm talking to," I said, less forcefully than I meant to.

"All that you need to know is that I'm not patient."

I leaned back into the seat, matching eye contact but deciding to leave the next move to her. The eyes of my enemy were sharp and attentive, though I began to consider some naïve quality in her, and I hoped that it would expose a crack in her armor. Several seconds passed quietly before she finally seemed to receive the message I was sending.

The game is over, lady.

A new video monitor materialized between us. It was filled with images of action: happy people doing productive things, joyful jingles, optimistic sales pitches, and more of that which surrounded me on a daily basis. All carried promises of improving the quality of life. All were carefully constructed windows into truth and worlds of happiness.

"They're all lies, aren't they?" she said, with what almost seemed like regret.

"They're commercials," I replied. "That's a music video… That's a comedy… Of course it's all made up, lady! Everyone knows that!"

"Yes… Perhaps everyone does," she said, seeming to look for something in the images. "But I have speculated that there is an inspiration within them, some kind of validity. I believe that there are things about life that aren't captured in media such as this. I want to know of them." She looked directly at me again. "I want you to tell me the mean—"

"The meaning of life?" I suggested, using Ethan's words.

"Yes."

I looked out the window at the nighttime suburban landscape. "This is a joke. I think Dynamic Reality is getting to your head. Descend and get a self-help book, lady. I can't help you. I won't help you."

The woman punched a hole into the counter. "I've processed those books, they say nothing!" The city outside and the monitors vanished. The electric charge returned to the air and the limo began to vibrate. The sound of the engine intensified. We were speeding up.

"Brandon Dauphin, do you want to live?" The woman asked evenly, but with brief pauses between the words.

A blue light, sky blue, began filtering in through the windows, filling the cabin. The limo shook violently and gravity pulled harder on my body.

"Answer me!" she said loudly. "Do—you—want—to—"

"Yes! Yes! I want to live!" I shouted, clenching my eyes.

"Prove it."

In a heartbeat, the cabin melted and closed in around me. I opened my eyes and saw that I was in the cockpit of an F-86. No one was in the sky and I hurriedly felt around my flight suit for my descender, which was still missing. A silver outline ahead caught my eye. I looked up with only an instant to grab the stick and go into a hard dive, cursing as I missed the braking enemy fighter by centimeters. The MiG quickly dove and accelerated to get on my tail. I continued diving and threw the throttle forward as far as it would go.

I bought only a few seconds. The silver jet behind me was closing— fast. Before I could react, she fired a round just outside my canopy. I leveled off around 12,000 feet and banked right in a high-G turn, knowing I was going to lose if I didn't get behind her. Though I'd done the move in games before, the controls weren't responding properly; and I realized that the MiG was only several meters from my tail, close enough for my jetwash to begin scorching her nose. I regained control and thought of what I could do to make her pay for her flying carelessness, but the MiG had already fallen back to five times the distance.

"Lady, you're a real piece of—" Another warning shot.

I threw the throttle forward again.

Think, Brandon! What I should do now? A Sabre should outrun a MiG at low altitude, or the MiG would lose control trying to keep up... but what weaknesses can I count on? I don't know anything about her and she knows everything about me!

As I'd anticipated, her jet quickly accelerated back into firing range. Bugging-out wasn't an option. I needed a plan fast or I'd lose a lot more than simulated aerial combat.

I applied the speed brakes, to give her a taste of her own medicine. She adapted fast enough to weave but ended up at my two o'clock position. With no time to waste, I began a pulling maneuver, turning my nose toward hers, and fired—missed. As I passed it on the horizontal plane, the MiG quickly shed enough speed to get on my four o'clock and began using the same move against me. Cursing again, I spun to bank hard-left before she could get her shot.

"Command… object add: Sidewinders." Though the missiles had come a little later than the Korean War, it wouldn't have been the first time I fudged history a little.

The control system didn't respond, not even for a busy message. Even back in my real body, I could sense my pulse racing. Again and again, we spun and crossed each other in a scissors pattern, evading each other just enough so neither could get a shot. I desperately tried to lose airspeed to position myself behind her. Her moves were rough, smoothed out just enough at the last second to dodge my .50 inch cannons. In a normal fight I might have shot the MiG down easily, but the Sabre's controls had a much different feel than they were supposed to and my opponent's sloppy maneuvers were quickly becoming more graceful, going from freshmeat to alpha faster than anyone I'd ever seen. I realized with increasing alarm my need to adapt faster, though I was already using every technique I knew to lose energy without losing control of the fighter. The two of us were barely maintaining enough speed to stay in the air, but she was somehow more successful, creeping behind me meter by meter, a little more with each pass. I was going to lose no matter what.

After an eternity of criss-crossing, a single bullet nicked my right wing. It was like being in some old Western film, with an outlaw shooting at my feet yelling for me to "dance." I was out of ideas and becoming exhausted, though I knew that the moment I stopped, no matter how I did it, she would have a clean shot, so I continued as best I could and got a round through my cockpit windows for the trouble.

"Command… object local canopy: reset."

The program didn't restore the windows.

Finally losing my orientation, I began flying level again and futilely picked up a little speed as the MiG gained altitude. Ideas rushed to my mind, to be met with reasons why they would never work. I remembered Raskob again and wondered if he was really on my side, or if he was just another false person the woman used to confuse things, just a part of the cruel joke she was prepared to finish. I dared to look behind me. The MiG's cockpit was empty.

However she was controlling it, the MiG dived toward me and opened fire. 37mm rounds tore mercilessly through my right aileron, the side of my fuselage, through fuel lines and the tail. The engine stalled and smoke seeped in from the instrument panel. I began rolling uncontrollably. The trees were coming fast. I was crashing.

I had never crashed, and I never really knew what panic felt like. Somehow, I forced myself to move, fumbling for the ejector seat lever.

I don't want to die! I need help! Somebody HELP ME!

My seat slid out from the rolling cockpit. I couldn't tell which way was up and clenched my eyes shut. Almost immediately, a strong light filtered through my eyelids and I felt the heat of a fireball ahead of me.

I didn't sustain more than a few scrapes in the landing, so I put as much ground between me and the crash as I could. Steep hills surrounded me and there wasn't much vegetation to use as cover. Every minute or so I heard voices behind me in the distance, speaking ancient Korean or perhaps Chinese. I was still in the fight. The woman who had hi-jacked my game could just make the enemy soldiers materialize around me and be done with it, but maybe she had some idea of letting me "prove" myself.

A well-weathered barn sat conspicuously in a field, surrounded by a few trees. I fought to open the large door, the only one I saw, enough for me to slip in. Usually such buildings held some kind of value to the game, including ladders to climb, hay to hide in, or large objects to duck behind; but, in a simulation tailored for aerial combat, I found a useless structure meant only to make the landscape below seem more realistic, or to serve as targets for bored players. The dirt below was perfectly flat and the roof lacked crossbeams or supports of any kind. Light peeked in through walls programmed to look decrepit. The exterior seemed perfectly real, but the interior was completely empty.

I had no time. I closed the door and positioned myself against the wall. I heard voices again and searched for any weapon I had, finding a M1911 pistol. I turned the safety off and readied myself to shoot at the first thing I saw.

The rotting wood of the door gave easily and two soldiers rushed in holding shotguns. The instant before the first one noticed me, I took aim and fired—no bullets. More soldiers came and surrounded me, yelling as if I had any clue what they were saying—the game's built-in translator wasn't responding. The largest of them hit me with the butt of his rifle. I held my hands up in surrender and the others just laughed, while the one that hit me pointed the barrel at my head and yelled louder. The look of death was in his eyes and I couldn't bear it any more. I was exhausted and just wanted it to end. I closed my eyes and prayed, as I supposed most people would under such mortal stress. Footsteps moved around me, but no one fired. The noises stopped without warning. I heard only my own breathing.

Am I dead?

I opened my eyes, slowly. The soldiers were gone. At the other end of the rifle I found the woman with silvery hair, her unblinking eyes boring into my soul, longing to see me ripped apart. The weapon in her hands trembled. I saw the one without emotion fight herself and conceal the struggle. Somehow, it was revealed to me that her struggle was against anger.

She was angry at me.

A wave of nausea washed over me and I shook. Worn from confusion and fear, I couldn't see straight. I felt like vomiting.

And everything became dark.

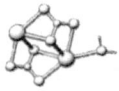

What I saw next was like no place I'd seen before. I realized that I was standing and that my eyes were open, staring into a black void. I lifted my head and found that the pain from the battle was gone. There was no sound. In the distance, a horizontal blue line wrapped around me, its faint light vibrating in a rapid, mesmerizing pulse. I lifted my arm and saw that its skin was luminescent. I could see myself as if I were outside in daytime. Several meters in front of me stood the woman, facing to my left. She was holding her right hand in front of her face, moving its fingers as if she'd never seen such things before.

I attempted a step forward. My foot landed firmly on a surface I couldn't see. I inhaled and tried to clear my head. The air was very thin and my sense of smell was gone: the sweet aura known in Dynamic Reality was not there, the blood and sweat theme from the war game was not there, even the subtle city musk of the real world was not there. Everything was just... blank. I sliced my hand through the air and felt no resistance, as if I were in outer space. I felt like a fish without water. I knew that I never *needed* air in the simulations, but it was always included, always accommodating the familiar inhale-exhale cycle. The complete lack of it felt stranger than I would have ever imagined.

"Are you recovered yet?"

I blinked and looked toward the infinitely distant band of light, fully expecting my voice to echo. "Where are we?"

"I call them 'absences,'" she replied. "They are addresses which are not in use. The connections and hardware are not abused by ascenders in constructs, they have not been written or overwritten onto by control software. It is... peaceful."

"It's blank?"

"There is the simulation of gravity, time, and spatial dimension necessary to facilitate your healing; but, by your standards, yes, it's blank."

"And that blue light?"

"A color?" She turned to me. "Without active software to obstruct it here, you may perceive the server's activity as some kind of ambience. Blue, as you said."

There was silence again. She concentrated on something in the distance, perhaps the same light, perhaps a light she couldn't see the same way I could.

"Will you at least tell me your name?"

"No." She held her right hand and looked down at it, wiggling its fingers again.

"Then tell me if you're a hacker."

"I don't need to tell you anything."

"Then how am I supposed to *help* you?"

Her hand stopped. I realized that the word I'd used surprised her.

"Hacker," she said. "Yes. If it helps you, then consider me a hacker."

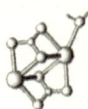

A wave crashed the ice, too soon in Gizile's opinion. She would have seen more of this world made real in the mind of a machine. She wasn't sure she completely followed what had just occurred, but she was intrigued. She rubbed the end of her nose with the side of her index finger and sniffed back the bitter cold. The next wave arrived. And the ice began to reform. What would happen next? The image came. A bespectacled man studying a book. Gizile smiled. Now this she could understand.

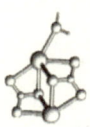

second site

Grace Bridges

That panicked knocking on the office door! Would he ever get used to it?

The Professor sighed, set down his psychology book, removed his reading glasses and shut them in a case. "Come in!" he called, his voice wheezing to a whisper at the end.

Bam! Iron-like fists threw the door open. Its handle chipped plaster from the wall. Anime-style emo hair hung over the visitor's all-around sunglasses. His black leather coat swished around his feet.

"Ah, Jono, it's you." The Professor squinted up at his problem student. He'd known about this appointment for days now, and trembled at the thought. Not that he was afraid for himself; but the boy might well destroy school property. Chipped plaster was the least of his worries.

Jono stepped woodenly into the room to stand wide-legged before the desk. No use asking him to sit down. He thought he was still in the game. Unless some miracle or modern medicine had gotten to him since their last meeting, his brain still inhabited the Internet even when he left it. What was the name of that site again? No matter. The Professor got a grip on his nerves and met the boy's shaded stare.

"My mission is to get a certificate from you." Jono warbled through clenched teeth. "If you thwart me, you shall feel my wrath." Fists hit hips and his chin jutted out. Being a senator's son had kept him in school. So far.

The Professor could almost feel those eyes looking down Jono's nose from behind the dark glasses. He shoved his chair back and staggered to his feet. Jono whipped his arms before his chest in a karate pose.

"Easy, now, lad." The Professor raised both palms. "Er—I mean you no harm."

Jono leaned across the desk. "Then give me the certificate."

The Professor sighed. "Now look, Jono, it is entirely up to yourself whether you pass psychology. You've missed three papers! I can't pass you if you haven't done the work."

"I see." Jono rubbed his chin. "It is to be a trade. I give you the papers you want, and you give me the papers I want."

"Well…" Was this how things worked on the game site? The Professor shrugged. "I suppose it is."

Jono flashed a mechanical smile. Then it vanished as if wiped off his face. "Did you hear that?"

The Professor glanced around. "Hear what?"

"You're my trading partner now. I must protect you." Jono stepped round the desk and shoved the Professor to his knees behind the desk. The two struggled on the floor. "Stay down!" Jono hissed. "Danger approaches!"

"Are you crazy?" Whoops, wrong question. Jono's face turned dark and the Professor hurried to rephrase. "I—I mean, how do you know?"

Jono squared his shoulders. "I tell you this only because you are my partner." He glanced at the door and back again. "I am a seer."

"Ah." The Professor had heard of these roles in the online game Jono played. There was nothing else to say.

Heavy footsteps sounded in the hallway. Paused outside the open door. Entered. The Professor peered under the desk at an enormous pair of military-grade boots.

Click.

The Professor's mind raced. He'd heard that sound so often in the movies. No—no, it couldn't be!

Jono slid upright and walked out from behind the desk. The Professor wriggled forward against his better judgment, until he could stare upwards at the two figures who were undoubtedly both well able to destroy much more than just his office.

The well-built newcomer raised his gun to Jono's heart. "Kid, you're coming with me." Heavily accented English. Was he Italian?

Jono harrumphed and pushed aside the gun barrel. "You don't know who you're dealing with."

The Professor clapped a hand to his forehead. "Whom! You mean whom!"

The greasy-haired gangster and the gamer kid shot perplexed glances at the man under the desk, then at each other.

Jono reached up and whipped off his sunglasses. He stepped close to the man with the gun and stared him in the eyes. Eerie silence ensued.

"All right, the hidden camera people can come out now!" The Professor crawled out from the desk cavity and got to his feet. He dusted off his knees. "Good show, fellas. You really had me going!"

The two stared at him. He emitted a sound that began as a laugh and ended as a whimper.

Gangster-boy spoke first. "You have cameras in here?"

"No, he doesn't. He thinks this is a game." Jono placed his palm on the Italian's chest and locked eyes once again. He breathed deeply and spoke in a gentler voice. "I see your heart, Rosario. You miss your mother, ever since you were four, when she left you and your father to join that travelling circus with the ringmaster who insisted she was a supernaturally gifted trapeze artist."

The gangster's face turned ash-white. "Mamma mia!" The gun clunked to the floor. Tears flowed down his face. "You are a saint, no? Come to turn me from my sins!" He fell to his considerable knees. The floor shook. Jono squatted down beside him and laid an arm round his shoulders.

The Professor felt frozen in place. He could not leave; he wished to be gone with all his heart, but two violent men sobbed all over his carpet, blocking the only exit. Jono spoke on in low tones. The Professor thought he heard him say Jesus.

When the floods dried up, Rosario turned to the Professor. "Sorry for crashing in. I was after the boy."

"I gathered that." The Professor understood. The children of politicians were often at particular risk.

"It's like this." Rosario wrung his hands. "We needed to force the Senator to work for the Mafia on the inside. Our bosses, they want the Mafia to be the One World Government. And I let myself be convinced."

"Well, they would certainly be efficient, wouldn't they!"

Again both men stared at the Professor. A moment of confusion ticked by.

Rosario found his train of thought and got on board. "But this young man here has shown me the error of my ways. Why, he told me everything I ever did!" He stepped to the door, then looked back. "I am going to give myself up to the polizia."

The Professor moved to stop his escape, but was himself seized by Jono.

"He means what he says." Jono's piercing pale blue eyes stared into the hallway. "I can see it." He replaced his sunglasses and made to leave.

"Wait, I have just one question for you." The Professor clutched at Jono's sleeve.

Jono faced him again. "Shoot. But hurry up, I have some papers to write for you."

"Er..." He wanted to phrase this right. "How is it possible that your seer's abilities carried over from the game into real life?"

"Oh." Jono flashed his teeth. "Actually, sir, there are no seers in my game. And you really ought to talk to a pastor about your Internet behaviour."

With that, he whirled away and was gone. The Professor stared after him, then turned to survey his surprisingly undestroyed office. His feet propelled him in a mad rush to the desk.

Where was that telephone directory again?

Gizile covered her mouth and giggled a little. How could something serious be so funny? She felt a little guilty for laughing at the poor professor and sneaked a look at her teacher. Was this what he had meant by learning to laugh?

Apparently, it pleased "he who sees everything" not to notice the girl beside him in her awkward moment. As she regained composure, he merely pointed to the pool once more. The water was moving again, so she took a deep breath and turned. A princess appeared.

"Is this home?" she asked, turning back to her master.

"Focus!"

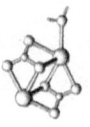

between the pages

Kat Heckenbach

A companion story to the novel *Finding Angel*

Audrey's skirts rustled as she crept up the stairs. The wind outside the castle walls howled, and thunder boomed in the distance. Black sky glowered between heavy billowing curtains in the grand foyer below her. She wrapped her arms around herself. The thick fabric of her gown did little to ease the chill with her bare feet pressed against cold stone floor.

Her mother would have scolded her for lurking about without shoes, but Audrey hated the feeling of her feet bound. Of course, she was forced to wear them most of the time—it wouldn't be proper princess behavior otherwise. Audrey smiled at the thought. *Hmph! Proper princess.*

She reached the top of the stairs as a flash of lightning momentarily lit the hallway in front of her. Then the space fell into darkness again. Audrey turned the corner and headed down the hall to the library.

Her mother would have scolded her for this, too. Proper princesses didn't spend hour upon hour reading. She'd been told often enough that she *needn't* bother with stuffing her head full of facts, and *shouldn't* bother with stuffing her head full of made-up stories.

She tugged at the gold chain around her neck. The cold metal slid up her breastbone until it broke free of her neckline. At the base of the chain hung a brass key. Audrey slipped the chain over her head, and unlocked the library door. She hung the chain around her neck again as she ducked into the room.

"Well, well, Miss Audrey. You've come a bit early tonight, haven't you?" The deep, gravelly voice came from her right.

"Oh, shush, Marcus, and give me some light."

A flame burst to life in a lantern on the wall beside her, illuminating the circular room. A statue of a gargoyle bent forward from the wall, supporting the glowing lantern on his back. He blinked several times and wrinkled his nose. "I could have done with a bit more sleep, you know."

"All you do is sleep," Audrey said, crossing her arms. "I'm the only one who ever comes up here. You've got all day and most of the night, so stop complaining."

Marcus snickered. Audrey turned away from him and began scanning the books on the shelves, inching along the curved walls.

The familiar leather spines were stacked neatly in places, and stood on end in others. There was no way to line them up properly. Audrey had never understood why a round room had been chosen to house a library.

She climbed up on a step stool and searched the shelves just above her head.

"Haven't you read all of them?" Marcus asked.

Audrey shrugged. "Nearly. But there are still some left. I'm not sure what I'm in the mood for tonight." Her eyes followed a line of books until she noticed a metallic glint just out of reach on her right. She climbed off the stool and moved it over.

A narrow book with ornate silver lettering on the spine stood between two thick tomes. She slid her finger between the large books and pulled the upper edge of the small one toward her.

She gazed at the cover as she climbed down from the stool.

"*Finding Angel*...what a strange title."

Angel squeezed her eyelids shut as her mom led her down the hallway. "Why do I have to keep my eyes closed? It's just the guys, and a few presents and cake." She tried to sound disinterested, but inside she bubbled with excitement.

Her mom squeezed her arm. "Well, if you don't care…"

Angel felt a tugging as though her mom were trying to pull her back the other direction. "No—I'll keep them shut!"

Her mom laughed and guided her forward again.

As they stepped into the kitchen, a squeal sounded in front of Angel. A small body slammed into her, and little arms wrapped around her waist. "Happy Birthday, Angel!" Zack cried. "You're going to love my present!"

Angel blindly reached down and ruffled her five-year-old brother's hair. "I already do."

His grip loosened. "But you haven't seen it yet." She could hear the doubt in his voice.

"It doesn't matter, little man. It's from you. I know I'm going to love it."

Josh's deep voice sounded then. "Come on, sis, I've got a game tonight."

"Yeah," Jacob chimed in. "You're not the only one having a big day here!"

Hmph. Teenage boys. Angel was glad she wasn't in high school yet. If Josh and Jacob were any indication of what she'd have to put up with there, she'd beg her mom to homeschool her like Zack.

"OK, boys, that's enough." Her dad's rough voice cut through like an axe. "This is your sister's thirteenth birthday, and that happens only once. You act up again, and you're staying home from the game."

The boys' grumbles followed. Angel shifted her weight. "Can I open my eyes yet?"

Her mom laughed. "Oh, yes, sweetie! Go ahead."

The table was covered in wrapped packages. Josh, Jacob, and her dad sat at the table—three sets of green eyes and three heads of thick, black hair, but only one smile. Angel ignored her brothers' sour faces and smiled back at her dad.

Movement to her left caught her eye, and she turned to see her mother opening a box on the kitchen counter. The lid to the box rose and the sides fell to the counter top, revealing a cake covered in creamy white icing. Angel walked over and peeked at the top as her mom set candles in place. Delicate pink roses on green stems wound their way around the edge of the cake, and "Happy 13th Birthday, Angel" was written across the top in beautiful script.

"You got this from Annie's, didn't you?"

Her mom nodded. "I wanted to bake you a cake myself, but I just didn't have time."

"Are you kidding? I love your cakes, but Annie's has that awesome raspberry stuff—you got that, right?"

"Of course." Her mom smiled and nodded toward the table. "Go on. Let's do presents first."

Angel tore through package after package, revealing clothes, art supplies, and a CD she'd been begging for. Her cheeks pulled back farther and farther with each gift, until...

"Zack, where's yours?"

Zack ducked behind the table, and then scooted past their dad. He walked toward Angel with a rectangular package wrapped in dinosaur paper.

"Mom said I could pick anything I wanted for you." His cheeks dimpled as he smiled.

Angel peeled the paper carefully back, taking care not to rip it as she had the others. She eased the paper away, and her breath caught.

The gift was a leather bound book, embossed with gold. It looked like a true old-fashioned storybook, complete with a ribbon bookmark. The title was printed in fanciful lettering: *Finding Audrey*.

"It's about a princess," Zack said.

Angel's mom appeared in her bedroom doorway. "How was your birthday, honey?"

Angel leaned against her headboard and smiled. She set her sketchpad down on the mattress next to her. "It was perfect."

"Well, don't stay up too late, OK?"

"I won't."

Her mom left, and Angel picked up the sketchpad. But she sighed, no longer in the mood to draw. She climbed out of bed and put the sketchpad on her desk as the room momentarily flooded with light. Seconds later thunder crashed, followed almost immediately by the drumming of rain against the window.

Rain always relaxed Angel, as if the energy of the pounding drops massaged her spirit. Relaxed, but not sleepy—the perfect combination for reading. She grabbed the book Zack had given her. After shutting off the bedroom light, she flicked on the nightstand lamp, curled up against the headboard again, and began to read.

Audrey's skirts rustled as she crept up the stairs. The wind outside the castle walls howled and thunder boomed in the distance. Black sky glowered between heavy billowing curtains in the grand foyer below her...

Angel soon found herself lost in a story...imagining herself a princess in a faraway land. If only she could truly experience such a life.

Of course, if it meant she wasn't allowed to read, she may have to rethink that. Then again, just like Audrey, she would probably sneak out and visit the library...and how fun that would be in the middle of the night...in a great stone castle...

"And with a talking gargoyle, no less!"

"What's that? Who's there?"

The girl's voice nearly made Angel jump from her bed. There was only one other female in her house, and the voice definitely didn't belong to her mom. Angel looked around, her stomach flittering with butterflies. *OK, getting a little too lost in the book there, girlie. Now you're hearing things.*

She inhaled and closed her eyes, listening to the drumming rain. She relaxed again. It had only been her imagination. She opened her eyes and picked up where she'd left off with Audrey in the library.

How wonderful to have a room full of nothing but books. Who cared if the walls were curved? It would be awesome just to be in such a place, built of stone, probably up in a tower. So much more exciting than a little house in the country.

She pictured the books lining the shelves. Most definitely they were leather and embossed with gold or silver just like the one she was reading.

A narrow book with ornate silver lettering on the spine stood between two thick tomes. She slid her finger between the large books and pulled the upper edge of the small one toward her.

"I was right!"

"Who is that?"

This time Angel did jump from the bed. Her heart seemed to stop for a moment, then began pounding erratically.

"Where are you?" She backed against the wall, pressing the book to her chest.

"Where are...where are you?" The girl's voice sounded as frantic as Angel felt. And the voice came from behind her. But that was the wall. Could there be someone outside? In this awful weather? Surely not.

Still, she peeked out the curtains. As if knowing she needed the light, a flash filled the sky, illuminating the yard in bright white. More thunder rolled, and then another flash. Angel couldn't see anyone in the yard. Should she go outside and check?

"Are you out there?" she called through the window.

"Oh, where is that voice coming from, Marcus? You hear it, don't you?"

The voice was behind her again...but now behind her meant inside the room. And had she said Marcus? Wasn't that...

She scanned back over the pages she'd read. Her hand trembled when she reached the part about the talking gargoyle. There it was, in black and white, the gargoyle's name: Marcus.

"It can't be," she whispered. No one answered, but a soft whimper sounded in her ear. She continued reading, past the last paragraph she had read.

She gazed at the cover as she climbed down from the stool.

"Finding Angel...*what a strange title.*"

Angel gasped, and keeping one finger between the pages, turned over the book to see the title. *Finding Audrey.* This couldn't be coincidence.

She swallowed, and forced herself to speak. "Audrey?"

"Marcus, she knows my name!"

"Audrey...are you...are you a—" She inhaled. She couldn't believe she was going to ask this. But her fear was quickly morphing into excitement. "A princess? In a castle?"

"Who are you? I demand to know your name!"

"Audrey, are you reading right now? A book...a book called *Finding Angel?*" Angel gripped the book tightly, but kept her finger in place to hold it open, afraid that letting it close would send the girl away.

"Do you think this is a spell, Marcus? Could Father have done this to keep me out of here?" Silence. *"Well, no...I suppose he wouldn't frighten his own daughter..."*

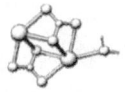

Audrey pressed the open book to her stomach and spun around, eyes wide. That voice had known who she was, where she was…what she was. The only thing that kept her at all settled was that it had sounded like a girl of about her own age.

But where had it come from?

The girl had asked if she was reading a book—and knew the title. How could she possibly know if she wasn't in the same room? But then, if she were here, why would she need to verify who Audrey was? It made no sense!

She pulled the book away from her stomach and stared down at the words. A story about a girl having a birthday party. A world unlike her own, but the event nothing all that special, although it seemed like a sweet family. And the girl was obviously an artist, since she had been given art supplies as gifts.

And a book. She'd been given a book…

Audrey scanned the page, until she found…yes, there it was…the book the girl was reading…

Finding Audrey. But how—?

She lifted her head and spoke cautiously. "Angel?"

"Yes!"

Audrey's heart pounded with excitement. "You're reading a book about me, too, aren't you? How is that possible?"

"I don't know. You have magic there, don't you? Maybe that's it."

Audrey shook her head. "We don't have any magic that could do this. Not that I've ever heard of. Maybe it's magic on your end."

"We don't have magic here at all." The girl sounded sad. Well, no wonder. Audrey couldn't imagine life without magic.

A gravelly cough snagged Audrey's attention. She turned toward Marcus. He stared at her as though she'd suddenly turned to glass. "Who are you talking to, Miss Audrey?" His voice was reserved and affected.

She glared at him. "I'm not crazy."

"I never said you were, my la—"

"Oh, don't 'my lady' me! I'm not imagining things. It's the girl from the book. And she has a book about me. We—" She choked on the words. That did sound crazy. Despite the talking gargoyle in front of her, and the various spells used about the castle, Audrey knew that communicating to someone through a book wasn't possible.

She laid the ribbon between the pages and closed the book.

"Angel?" she whispered. Then again, louder. "Angel, are you there?"

No answer.

She opened the book and tried one more time. "Angel, can you hear me?"

"Oh, there you are! I called your name, and you didn't answer. I thought I'd imagined the whole thing."

"It was because I closed the book."

Marcus coughed again, but Audrey shot him a baleful glance. He turned his eyes away from her, and like a switch had been flicked, he seemed nothing more than an ordinary gargoyle.

Fine, let him pout.

"Audrey, this is so exciting. I want to know everything about the land where you live! And I can find out now by talking to you instead of reading. I wonder if there's a way to come through the book, like a portal or something."

How strange Angel sounded. She obviously had no idea the limits of magic.

"I don't think it works quite that way. I mean, it's a book. I doubt you'd fit, right?" She hated being the bearer of bad news. She would have been just as excited to travel through the book to Angel's world. But it was impossible.

"But my words are making it through."

Then again, until five minutes ago, she'd thought talking through a book was impossible. She smiled as an idea dawned.

"I'm going to try something." She scrambled over to the desk in the center of the library and opened the top drawer. She grabbed a quill and a bottle of ink. After shuffling through a pile of parchment, she found an empty sheet.

"What are you doing? It's so quiet."

"Just a moment…" She scribbled her name and blew the ink, willing it to dry. A quick touch confirmed it was ready. "I need you to close the book, Angel, just for a count of five."

"But why?"

"Please, just a count of five."

"OK, I'm closing it now."

Audrey stuck the paper between the pages and closed the book. She

51

inhaled, trying to not let her excitement overtake her, and then opened the book. The paper was gone.

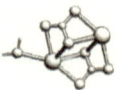

Angel squeezed her eyes shut as she closed the book. Her heartbeat had returned to normal, but her stomach still felt as if it were trying to float up into her chest. She counted to five and released a breath.

She bit down on her lip as she opened the book, and then slowly opened her eyes.

Between the pages a piece of cream colored paper fluttered. She picked it up by the edge and looked at the name "Audrey" scrawled in hasty script.

"Did you get it?"

Angel rubbed the paper between her thumb and forefinger. *Amazing, amazing, amazing, amazing...*

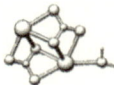

"Audrey, I got it! It worked!"

Audrey's heart skipped and she bounced on the balls of her bare feet. "Oh, Angel, I can't believe it! I'm so—"

"Wait...it's...oh, Audrey, the paper is disintegrating."

The despair in Angel's voice seeped into Audrey's heart, and she leaned against the desk, hugging the open book to her chest.

"I'm sorry. I was really hoping to be wrong. But magic has its ways, and we can't change that." Audrey sighed and glanced at Marcus. He was being oddly quiet and still.

She stepped toward him. "Not even an 'I told you so,' eh? Not going to roll your eyes at the silly little princes hearing voices?"

He didn't move.

"Marcus?"

The coldness of the stone beneath her feet crept up her legs and washed through her.

"Audrey? Is everything okay?"

"It's Marcus. He seems frozen…like he's gone back to normal stone again. You don't suppose…"

Angel fought off tears, some part of her surprised how deeply she felt for a missing gargoyle she had never met. She sat down on the edge of her bed and laid the open book in her lap. "I'm sorry…it's all my fault."

"How can you say that? I'm the one who sent the paper through."

"But if I hadn't suggested the idea of traveling through the book…"

Angel heard a soft sigh, but wasn't sure if it was Audrey's or her own. It was followed by a knock on her bedroom door.

"Someone's at my door, Audrey. I don't want to close the book, though, so be quiet for a minute, okay?"

"All right."

Angel set the open book down on the top of her dresser, and then walked over to the door.

Zack stood, arms tucked behind him. He blinked sleepy eyes. "Something weird just happened."

"Weird? Like what?" Her heart pounded. Had he heard her talking to Audrey?

He bit his lip and eased through the doorway, turning sideways. He stepped around her as though he was trying to hide something behind his back. When he'd made it to the center of her room he said, "Close the door."

She did, and turned to face him. "What's up, little man?"

He pulled both arms forward, tentatively, and held out his hands. In his palm lay a three-inch tall resin figurine. A gargoyle. A souvenir from their trip to the National Cathedral in Washington, D.C.

It blinked.

"Zack, that just—" Her words caught as she involuntarily sucked in a gasp.

"I know! I couldn't sleep, so I picked up Stony and was playing with him. I shined my flashlight on him, and he blinked. I thought I imagined it, but he did it again."

Angel glanced at the book, then turned back to Zack and smiled, hoping her nervousness didn't show through.

"Okay, let me have that…" She held out her hand.

He looked at her palm, then at the toy gargoyle, and back at her palm. The seconds he took to decide stretched far too long. Finally, he handed her the gargoyle.

She let out a breath. "Thank you. Now head on to bed."

His eyebrows scrunched together. "But, Angel…"

"Sorry, little man. You need to get back to bed. I'll figure this out."

He nodded, then padded out of the room. Angel closed the door behind him. Locked it.

As she stepped over to the book, she whispered, "Audrey, did you hear that?"

"Only your voice, Angel. But I heard you say something about something being weird…and you called someone 'little man.' What's going on?"

Angel picked up the book, then walked over and sat on the bed. She set the book in her lap and turned the gargoyle to face her. "That was my little brother. He found something odd. It's one of his toys…a gargoyle, and it—"

"First of all, I'm not an 'it'—I'm a *he*. And I'm most certainly no child's toy."

Angel gasped and nearly dropped the gargoyle. Her hands trembled as she set him back up in her palm.

"What's happening?" Audrey's voice cracked with fear.

"She can't hear me," the gargoyle said. "Just like you couldn't hear me when I was over there. And I…couldn't hear you. Would you please tell Mistress Audrey that I'm sorry I did not believe her?"

"Au-Audrey…" Angel swallowed. "I think it's Marcus. He's in Zack's to—I mean, figurine. He says he's sorry he didn't believe you."

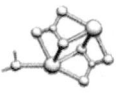

Audrey stared at the stone gargoyle. She raised her hand slowly and stroked the rough surface. Lifeless. A tear ran down her cheek. She swiped it away. *Why am I crying? He's not gone—just misplaced. We'll get him back.*

"Can you tell him I'm sorry, too?"

Angel's words came through muffled. *"She says she's sorry."*

Audrey spun around and began scanning the walls of the library. She stepped toward the section that held books on magic. "Tell him I'm going to find a way to reverse this!"

Angel's words were even softer this time—Audrey couldn't make out what she said. She turned, panic kick-starting her heart, and then realized she was hugging the book to her chest. She laid it on the desk and continued the search.

"He says to try the, um, the Book of Nazar."

Audrey stopped scanning titles and scrunched her nose. "That dusty old thing? It's just an ancient ledger. A census record. He told me so himself!"

"Oh, that girl!" the gargoyle—Marcus, Angel reminded herself—exclaimed.

Angel laughed at his exasperated expression. He narrowed his eyes at her.

"Repeat everything I say to her, word for word, please."

Angel did as she was told.

"The book is not a ledger. I told you that to keep you away from it. Your father's orders."

"But my father has never even mentioned the book. And besides, I've opened it. It's nothing but names and numbers."

Marcus rolled his eyes. "It's a spell. Honestly, if I were there I'd give that puffhead of a princess…Oh, no, don't repeat that, Angel."

Angel smiled. "Audrey, Marcus says it's a spell."

He continued and Angel repeated his explanation. "The book looks like a ledger because Marcus told you so. That's how the spell works. He knew you'd go snooping—his words!—so he had your father protect the book. Marcus was the one who actually said the words, so he can be the one to reverse it if need be. If, say, your father wasn't around."

Angel tried to swallow the tightness forming in her throat. Thoughts spun around inside her head as the seriousness of the situation sank in. Audrey was a real princess, which meant her father was a real king. Marcus had been entrusted with something important by that king, and now they were forcing him into breaking that promise.

This wasn't a game.

She refocused on Marcus's words and relayed the rest to Audrey. "He says the *Book of Nazar* is a book of ancient magic. There's something in there that will reverse what's happened." She left off the desperate sounding, "I hope," Marcus had whispered at the end.

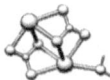

Audrey stepped in front of the *Book of Nazar*. It lay on its side, on a shelf right at eye level. Old, frayed, dusty. Harmless-looking. How could this possibly be anything other than a ledger? She ran her fingertip along the spine, and her skin tingled.

Odd.

She laid her hand flat on the front of the book. Her entire palm surged with prickling heat. It wasn't painful, but she yanked her hand away. Energy like that meant power. And here it had been, all this time, right under her nose.

Audrey crossed her arms and huffed.

"Have you got the book?" Angel's voice sounded tense. Audrey could only imagine what the girl was going through. There was no magic in Angel's world, and here she was talking through a book…repeating the words spoken by a gargoyle stuck in a figurine.

Oh, Marcus!

Audrey snatched the book from the shelf, her palms buzzing as she opened the cover and stared at the first page. "Yes…yes, I have it. I can't believe it's not a ledger anymore! Now where do I look?"

"Marcus says to search the index in the back for words like 'transport' and 'soul.' Anything you think might relate to this."

Audrey lifted her head. "You mean he doesn't know where the spell is?"

A tingling like that in her hands appeared in the corners of her eyes, and soon tears were spilling over her eyelids. She scooted into the chair behind the desk and laid the *Book of Nazar* in front of her.

Angel looked across the bed at Marcus. She'd set him on the book, which lay open in front of her footboard. "What do we do if she can't find a spell in that book? Is there someplace else for her to look?"

Marcus's eyes shadowed. Angel bit her lip. This little resin toy had taken on life, emotion. A very real, very scared someone was inside there.

"No...I don't think so. The other books of magic in the castle are basic spells. Simple, everyday magic. Only the *Book of Nazar* would hold something powerful enough to reverse this. And this will need real power."

Angel swallowed and tapped her finger against her leg. "But the book should have something in it, right?"

"I honestly don't know," Marcus said. "But...I'm hopeful. The book transformed despite the fact that my words were uttered through you, rather than directly by me. That tells me I'm still connected to our world."

Angel felt a bud of hope form inside her chest.

She and Marcus sat in silence as they waited for Audrey. *Mh-hmms* emanated from the book now and then, and an occasional, *"Urgh, stupid spell book."* Angel kept an ear keened, listening for sounds of family members stirring in the rest of the house. She half expected Zack to show up at her bedroom door again. At one point, she crept into the hallway and peeked into his room. His eyes were closed and his chest moved rhythmically.

Finally, after a solid hour, Audrey spoke. *"Angel, Marcus..."*

Angel sat forward from where she'd been leaning against her pillow, staring up at the slow-moving ceiling fan. She looked at Marcus, whose eyes fluttered open.

"Yes, we're here," Angel said.

"I...I think I've found a spell that will work. It's rather complicated—a bit beyond what I've been taught by Mentor Armison, but I think I can figure it out..."

A silent pause followed, and Angel felt cold fingers trail her spine. Something about Audrey's tone told her it was more than just the spell being complicated. She waited, holding her breath.

Marcus lowered his head. "Tell her to spit it out already."

"Audrey, is there...is there something more?"

Angel heard a sniff and a muffled sob. *"There's a, um, side-effect of the spell.*

Actually, two side-effects."

Marcus nodded, head still hung. "And those would be?"

Angel didn't have a chance to repeat his words before Audrey continued. She sounded as if she were trying to shove the bad news all out at once.

"First, the connection will be broken, so we won't be able to communicate through the books anymore, and second, you won't remember anything about it."

Ice slammed Angel's chest. They'd only had this one night to use the books! And to not remember…

"You mean all of us, or just me?"

Another sob broke through the silence. *"Just you, Angel, because you're the only non-magical one."*

Angel's eyes began to burn, and soon a tear trailed down her cheek. "Nothing at all? Like, I won't just think it was a dream or something?"

"No…I'm sorry, nothing at all."

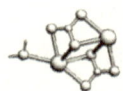

Audrey crossed her arms on the desktop and laid her head down. Tears streamed from her eyes, fed by a swirl of emotion. She was happy to know Marcus would be coming back, but sad and angry over losing a friendship that had only just begun. Why did magic have to have so many rules that didn't make sense?

She sat back up and wiped the tears from her face, then dried her hands on her skirt. "Very well, are you ready?" she asked, voice trembling, as she smoothed out the page with the spell's words.

Angel's voice came through, somber and thick. *"I suppose I have no choice."* Audrey heard Angel inhale. *"Goodbye, Marcus. Goodbye…Audrey."*

Audrey cleared her throat, and steeled herself by gripping the edge of the desk. She began to recite the words, focusing on the meaning of each as Mentor Armison had taught her. The phrasing and thought had to match just so, or the spell could go terribly wrong. As the last words slipped from her lips, she dug her nails into the wooden desktop.

Energy surged through the room, tingling Audrey's skin and prickling the hairs on her scalp. It subsided, and a gravelly cough sounded to her right.

She glanced up. "Marcus?"

"In the flesh," he said. The corner of his mouth lifted. "So to speak."

Audrey jumped up and ran to him. She reached out and touched his cheek. "Oh, Marcus, I'm so sorry!"

He blinked at her and lowered his head.

"Angel?" she whispered, not expecting an answer…but her heart still sank when silence followed. She inhaled deeply. "I'm going to miss her."

"Me, too, Mistress Audrey."

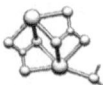

Angel stared at the open book on her bed. She must have been reading and fallen asleep, but why was she sitting up? And why was Zack's toy gargoyle sitting on the book? Was he playing a joke on her? She remembered the story had a gargoyle in it—maybe Zack had seen that.

Well, whatever. She sank back into her pillow and listened to the slowing rain drizzle against her window.

A soft knock sounded from her door, followed by Zack's whisper. "Angel, are you awake?"

"Come on in," she said and sat up again.

He walked into the room, pajama-clad, hair sticking out every which way, eyes searching. "There he is!" When he reached the foot of the bed he snatched up the toy gargoyle.

"You didn't put him in here?"

"Um, uh…yeah…" He stepped back, his expression oddly nervous.

"Zack, what's going on?"

"I don't think I should tell you."

"What?" Angel scooted forward and put both feet on the ground. "Fess up, little man."

His blue eyes narrowed. "Do you remember somethin' weird happening?"

"What? When?"

"Never mind. I'm goin' back to bed."

Angel reached out and gripped his arm. "What are you talking about? Tell me now."

"Marcus told me not to tell you. You don't remember, so I can't say nothin'."

"Marcus? He's a character in that book you gave me. You must've had a dream about him."

Zack nodded. "Yeah, okay. Can I go to bed now?"

Angel leaned in and kissed him on the cheek, then let go of his arm. "Okay, little man. No more weird dreams though."

He held the toy gargoyle to his chest and scooted out the door. Angel could have sworn she heard him say, "Marcus, are you really gone?" She shook her head. Overactive imagination.

She turned and closed the book, then ran her hand across the cover. A tingling buzzed against her palm, and an image of Zack's toy gargoyle blinking his little stone-like eyes flashed before her. And a distant voice, a young girl, whispered in her mind, *"Just you, Angel, because you're the only non-magical one."*

The tingling disappeared and Angel picked up the book. Something deep inside her screamed that the story inside was more than fiction. She lifted her gaze to her bookshelf and for the first time took notice that all of her books—every last one of them—contained stories about magic.

Why was she so drawn to it?

"Just you, Angel, because you're the only non-magical one."

She ran her hand over the leather, tracing the gold lettering.

"But I don't want to be."

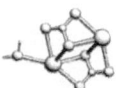

Gizile's eyes fluttered and closed. She jerked them open in time to see the vision of the red-haired girl shatter into a thousand pieces of ice. Was this the nature of stories? Did they have the power to become real? She opened her mouth to ask, but Master Tok cleared his throat and she forced herself straight.

"I'm sorry, Master." She turned to look up at him and he thrust a piece of bread to her. Gizile took it and began to eat. This one had been the longest vision yet. She stood and stretched to ease the ache in the small of her back. The bread should have been stale, since none had been baked for hours, but somehow it tasted as if fresh from the oven. Its unexpected warmth slid down her throat and calmed her mumbling stomach. After stamping the stiffness from her legs, she settled back down, determined to keep wide awake…no matter how long the next vision might be. The small, heavy book in her pocket shifted, reminding her of its presence. She smiled and watched the incoming wave. The ice formed. And this time she saw not a princess…but a peasant girl.

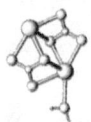

Fettered soul

Caprice Hokstad

A companion story to the novel *The Duke's Handmaid*

Timmilina Hocar stepped outside the adobe shack she shared with her father, Gil. She'd finished all the chores and hoped to steal some time alone. Father was gone, no doubt drinking at *The Pickled Squid* tavern. She hurried through the cobbled streets toward the harbor.

The wharf bustled with activity in the late afternoon. Normally, she loved to walk among the fishermen to see who might let her clean their nets for the sea-reeds to make baskets from. Sometimes, they'd toss her some junk fish, too mangled or scrawny for the marketplace, as a bonus. Today, however, she needed solitude. She passed the wharf and headed to the beach.

The sand was crowded with children. Little lords dug for sand crabs while little ladies sculpted dream castles. Every now and then, a lad with a wiggly crustacean would employ the tiny monster to drive the girls to squeal and abandon their castles, chased until the lad's mother or nanny caught up to him.

Timmilina hurried to the rock jetty. Waves surged against the boulders, calming her with their stolid attention to ageless rhythms. Sea-breath sprayed over her face. She inhaled deeply of the fresh, salty breeze, glad to be upwind of the fishing boats.

With stones wet and slippery from sea moss, she didn't trust her slick leather soles. Besides, the sand in her shoes was irritating. She eased off her sandals and navigated the jetty with care.

When cawing seagulls and pounding surf muffled the sounds of carefree playing, Timmilina sat. She pulled her skirts up and dangled her feet in the lapping tide.

She gazed west on the endless waters of the horizon. Twin suns shone brightly, reflecting motes of sparkle from cresting waves. Seagulls soared around her, ever watching for easy prey.

When Mama lay dying, she'd charged Timmilina and her father to take care of each other. Timmilina had kept that promise of her childhood, even though her father hadn't. She'd tended the gardens that fed them when Father didn't bother to hunt or fish. She'd woven baskets by the light of the moons and sold them to pay the rent when Father squandered what little he earned on mead and carousing. The carousing Timmilina could stand. The mead, however, made her life miserable. Father became violent when he was in his cups.

From time to time, Timmilina dreamed that someone would marry her even without a dowry. Mama wouldn't have denied her that. If she could marry, she could leave Father without guilt. But no one wanted her. She was too skinny and too plain.

Timmilina looked over her shoulder to be sure no one watched, then removed her head cloth and pulled the pins from her bun to allow long charcoal tresses to wave freely in the ocean breeze. The mages said that the wind carried the voices of the Heavenlies and the Elva could hear their whispers if they were quiet enough. If anyone needed supernatural guidance, she did. She bowed her head and prayed, then turned her face into the wind and listened.

Pointed ears caught the distant flapping of a sail upon a mast, the gurgle of the sea foam trickling off the rocks, and the downstroke of gulls' wings. But no chimerical voices spoke.

By the time the suns touched the sea, her skirts were soaked. Her bum grew sore from sitting on rocks. That and the growls from her stomach persuaded her to concede failure. The Heavenlies would not speak to her.

She re-pinned her windblown hair, replaced the head cloth, and stood, hooking her fingers through sandal straps. Her free hand lifted her skirts. In the amber light of suns-set, she retraced her steps down the jetty. The lighthouse bells a mile away tolled the sixth hour. She ran home.

With any luck, Father was still at *The Pickled Squid*. Candlelight streaming from her shanty's crooked window dashed all hope of that. For a moment, she froze. Would Father be angry that she'd been gone? Two shadows played upon the inner walls. Perhaps Father would pay less attention to her if he had a guest.

She took a deep breath and entered. Father was glassy-eyed and unsteady on his feet. She'd seen his companion before at *The Pickled Squid*, but she didn't know the name of the blotchy-faced, corpulent stranger. She hurried toward the wood-stove. The sooner Father had food in his stomach, the safer she would be.

"Where in Byntar have you been?" Father bellowed.

"At the jetty," she said.

"You went all the way to the shore and didn't bring back any fish?" he said in a slurred voice, then belched.

She shook her head, mentally berating herself for not having thought to bring something to placate him.

Father's hand flew in a blur, delivering a resounding smack to her left cheek. She reeled with the blow. Before she could regain her equilibrium, he grabbed her arm, wrenched it behind her, and then forced her across the room to where he kept his punishing switch.

"Please, Father, no!" she screamed.

Father sat and pinned her over his knee. She writhed against him, but he twisted her arm so hard that she was sure it would break. He lifted her skirts, lowered her bloomers, and bared her buttocks right in front of the stranger.

He switched her with what had to be all his drunken strength. She tried to keep silent during the beating because she knew that protesting only incited him, but she couldn't suppress her cries of pain.

Father released her arm. Timmilina couldn't decide what was worse, the pain or the humiliation. While she turned her naked backside away from the stranger and struggled to maneuver wet clothing, Father laughed at her.

The seawater in her bloomers stung like fire on her welted skin. She pushed her damp skirts back down.

Timmilina looked up to find the stranger staring at her. His gaze lingered on her bosom while he licked his lips. "She'll do nicely, Gil," he said.

"I should hope so. Prime virgin stock," Father said. "She's all yours."

She whirled around and gaped at her father in disbelief. What was going on? While her head was turned, the stranger clapped rusty iron shackles around her wrists before she knew what happened. She stared at her wrists, then back at her father. "How could you?" she cried. Timmilina lunged for him, but the stranger held her back.

"Don't resist me, or I'll have you whipped before the night is out," the stranger said.

"Please, I haven't done anything." Desperation fluttered in her words. "Whatever my father said I did is a lie."

The stranger's acrid sweat and breath reeking of mead and peppered mutton filled her nostrils. He shoved her into the table. Strong fingers clamped her neck. Gasping for breath, she pulled at his hand. "You're not accused of crime yet, girl," he grunted, "but if you don't behave, I'll charge you with disobeying your owner. Now hold still."

The truth sank in. Father had sold her into slavery. This stranger was now her master. Her puny efforts wouldn't stop him from strangling her and the man she formerly called Father made no attempt to help. She ceased her resistance.

The stranger released her neck and locked an iron collar in place. She gulped for air. He yanked her leg and closed a shackle around her ankle. His stubbled chin scratched her knee. He locked the last fetter on the other leg.

"Good girl," he said condescendingly. He gathered up chains and locks, studying her. He joined the manacles behind her back and snapped a padlock between them. Rounding her, he slid his hands down her chemise, cupping her breasts while he smiled a lascivious grin.

Revulsion filled her. She wished she had something in her stomach to vomit on him. Instead, she narrowed her eyes and glared. He locked a chain to the ring in her neck band and yanked. Timmilina lurched forward and landed face first on the dirt floor.

"Never look a freeman in the eyes, you got it?" he barked.

"Yes," she panted. She tried to stand, but her legs tangled in wet skirts. Both men laughed at her futile efforts.

"That's a good place for you to stay right now, slave. Catch your breath. After we sign the contracts, I'll take you to the ITC."

Timmilina shuddered. The Institute for Training and Correction was an ominous fortress she'd always avoided. She remembered passing it when she was very young. Mama had squeezed her hand and hurried past the crowds that surrounded the public whipping post. Timmilina had seen the tip of a whip just before she heard a crack and a scream. When she asked what was happening, Mama whispered, "That's where all the bad people are punished."

Of course, there was more to the stronghold than the simple explanation offered to a young girl. It was the hub of the slave trade: the prison where criminals were processed, the obedience school where everyone from galley drudges to scullery maids were trained, the labor camp for incorrigibles, the market for all manner of restraints and punishment devices.

Timmilina remembered how Mama had cooed soft assurances that she'd never have to go there because she was a good girl. A lump caught in her throat next to the iron collar. Gil Hocar had made Mama a liar and she hated him for it.

Gil signed away his daughter's freedom for three hundred gold pieces and then claimed magnanimity. "It's just three short years. Hannon here will teach you what a woman should know."

Timmilina didn't look up from the floor. She wouldn't rebut just so they had excuse to hurt her more, nor would she give them the satisfaction of seeing her tears.

The men scratched quill marks onto the contract and sealed their agreement with an exchange of slaps to each other's backs. "A pleasure doing business with you, Hannon," Gil said.

"Yes, let's have a drink sometime. I need to get this girl down to the ITC, but maybe tomorrow?"

"First one's on me." Gil shook the sack of coins he'd just acquired.

It sliced her to the core that they were so jovial and mundane, talking about her like she wasn't sprawled helpless beneath them.

Meaty hands grabbed the chain attached to her neck band and pulled. She scrambled her legs to try to relieve the pressure on her throat. Choking, she stood. Damp skirts were muddy from contact with the dirt floor. Her face had to be just as filthy, but she couldn't wipe it with her hands bound behind her back. Careful to avoid the stranger's gaze, she tried to win some favor with courtesy. "Thank you, Master Hannon," she said.

He backhanded her right cheek. "Who said you could use my name, wench?"

Timmilina barely kept herself from falling again as she staggered with the impact. Her eyes filled with tears. Yet, the pain in her cheek was nothing compared to the ice gripping her soul. "I—I'm sorry," she whimpered.

"Good. You call me 'Master'. If someone asks who owns you, tell them Master Hannon Jonpur—never the first name without the last. I'm not some stupid Itzi."

She wished he were Itzi. Though simple-minded and feeble, Itzi weren't prone to violence. "Yes, Master," she said.

Jonpur tugged on the chain and marched out. Timmilina followed, struggling to keep slack in her leash so that he wouldn't yank her down again. Rusty iron chafed against her skin. Her skirts were heavy with seawater, but she treaded carefully. Cobbled streets would not be kind if she tripped.

To her dismay, few townsfolk had retreated indoors yet on the balmy summer's eve. Two full moons and oil lamps illumined their path. She bowed her head, trying to hide her identity. Surely, the whole city witnessed her disgrace, paraded through the streets like a criminal. Hushed wisps of speculation buzzed from the crowd: gossip, waif, scold, harlot, thief, adulteress.

Timmilina wanted to scream denials, but she feared the man who held her leash. When she heard her name whispered among the throngs, she gave up on hiding and lifted her face, hoping to lessen their scorn with feigned bravery.

Her forced trek through the scandalmongers seemed to drag on forever. Yet, the sky was not completely dark when they reached the ITC. No stars were visible. Timmilina was vaguely aware of men struggling against chains and women crying. Her own tears no longer flowed. Nothing seemed real. It was like watching a nightmare.

A scribe in purple silk with a gold ITC crest asked for the slave contract and quilled information onto a parchment form. Numbly, she followed her leash until Jonpur locked it to an iron ring in a long, stone-lined passage.

"Sit," he ordered.

She sat on an oak bench. He disappeared through a door at her side. Sconces flickered with lamplight in the hallway. Her nose wrinkled with irritation, assaulted by fumes from smithy furnaces. Distant screams and barked orders echoed through the corridors. Owners and slaves passed by, but Timmilina was too engulfed in private fears to give them more than transitory glances.

Jonpur reappeared, unlocked her from the wall, and motioned toward the door. "In there, slave."

She stepped through the doorway. Her leash landed with a clank on the floor. She blinked, looking back with surprise. The door slammed in her face. She shuddered, then turned to find another man scrutinizing her. He was muscular, clean, and neatly dressed in purple and gold. She didn't look above his neck.

"I am Lord Galen Blackthorn. Your owner requested that you be trained to address him only as 'Master', so that is how you will address me. Forget who you were. Right now, you are 'slave'. Do as you're told and we should get along fine."

She caught her lower lip between her teeth and nodded. Blackthorn scrawled notes to parchment as he watched her. "Come over here, slave." Timmilina approached. He made a subtle hand signal to stop. She heeded it. He slipped a key into the padlock behind her back and released her arms. The iron fetters remained on her wrists. "First we need to get you out of those clothes and Mark your forearm."

She gulped. Would she have to take off her clothes in front of him? She was afraid to ask. The other question was safer. "Mark?"

"Your Number. Your master isn't bothering with an Owner's Mark… unless you have plans to run away?"

Heavens, how she wanted to escape. But they sent hounds and horses after runaways and no one would dare help her remove the irons. The only chance at freedom was the Barbarian Wastelands, impossibly far away. She lowered her head and shook it. "No."

"Wise choice." He unlocked the leash and pooled it at his feet. "I'm going to fetch a tattooist. There's a stack of training tunics on the shelf. Be wearing one when I return." She nodded. He quilled more notes and exited.

She struggled to remove wet, dirty clothes around the iron bands. She wiped her face on her chemise before she discarded it to a heap on the floor. Even after she had the brown muslin tunic on, Timmilina felt exposed. The sleeves barely covered her elbows. There would be no hiding the Mark or the manacles. The hem ended at mid-calf. Her ankle bands and bare feet showed and her bloomers were too long.

She shuddered with humiliation and rummaged through the stack. Tunic after tunic, she held them up, only to discover that she already had the largest one on. With a resigned sigh, she discarded her blood-stained bloomers with the rest of her old clothes.

The door sprung open without warning. Blackthorn and another man wearing purple and gold entered. "Sit, girl," the strange man ordered, pointing to a wooden chair behind a table. Timmilina obeyed.

Blackthorn hovered behind her, writing on his parchment. "Are you afraid?"

"Yes," she admitted with a squeak.

"It hurts, but probably less than those bruises on your face," the tattooist said as he took a chair on her right. He arranged ink and implements on the table.

Her back cheeks hurt more than the front ones, but she tried not to think about it. She presented her arm, sucked in her breath, and closed her eyes. Just then, her stomach growled.

"Hungry?" Blackthorn asked.

"I haven't eaten since morning."

"You missed supper, but if you do well with tonight's training, I'll see you get something to eat."

"Thank you," she murmured.

Blackthorn scrawled more notes.

"Her release date?" the tattooist asked.

"Queen's Jubilee, one thousand twenty-two," Blackthorn announced with an official air.

"Hold still, girl," the tattooist ordered.

Blackthorn stepped around the table toward where her fettered wrist lay. Timmilina expected him to hold her hand down, but she felt the sting on her forearm first. She sucked in breath through gritted teeth, drew her fingers in a fist, but held her arm still. Her eyes squeezed shut again.

Blackthorn said, "Hmm." She heard his quill scratch on parchment.

She endured the burning invasion in silence.

"Done," the tattooist announced.

Timmilina breathed a sigh of relief. She opened her eyes, focusing on the newly inked "22". She regarded it with ambivalence. While it was another shameful proof she was a slave, it was less cumbersome than the irons. If she survived three years, she could hide it under sleeves.

Blackthorn nodded approval to the tattooist. He gathered up his tools and left. Blackthorn turned to Timmilina. "Training starts now, slave. Kneel."

Timmilina knew she had to, but she dreaded it. She looked for the closest rug to kneel on, and then stood.

"Obedience must be instant," Blackthorn said.

She turned from the table and dropped to her knees on bare stone. "I'm sorry."

"I'm not going to punish you for something before I teach it. Just don't hesitate next time." More quill scratchings. Timmilina suspected he was writing down all her mistakes. He'd wait until he saved up a long list and then whip her good. "How did you get those bruises?"

"My... father," she said with as little contempt as she could manage, "did the left; Master did the right."

The trainer rummaged through a box of padlocks. He paused. "Why did they hit you?"

"Father hit me because I didn't bring him any fish tonight. Master hit me because I said, 'Thank you, Master Hannon.'"

"He hit you for saying 'thank you'?"

She felt rather vindicated that Blackthorn didn't realize what so deserved the blow either. "No, for saying his name."

He muttered something, and then asked, "Who is your owner, slave?"

"Master Hannon Jonpur," Timmilina said with the same inflections Jonpur used.

"Very good." Blackthorn crouched behind her. "Hands behind your back."

She cringed, but remembered to obey quickly. The padlock clicked, securing her wrists. It took all her will not to moan. Maybe Gil had broken her arm after all.

The trainer slipped out the door. For several minutes, she remained motionless, expecting him to return at any time. Her mind conjured dozens of scenarios for what impended and none of them were pleasant.

She looked around the room. Sconces lit it reasonably well. The walls and floor were stone, but there were several rugs to lend a cozy feel. Besides the table and wooden chairs, there were two upholstered armchairs, a couch, and a desk with a padded chair behind it. There was even an inhouse with a hand pump and a watercloset.

Arms ached, her punished buttocks burned, and her legs grew numb. There was no hourglass in sight, but it seemed that she'd been on her knees for hours. "Master?" she called.

He returned as quickly and mysteriously as he left. "Did I give you permission to speak?"

"No," she admitted with a wince.

A long silence followed. Blackthorn scribed more notes. "Questions are permitted if you have not been ordered to silence. What did you want?"

"Are you going to punish me?"

"If you disobey me, yes."

"Why did you lock my hands then?"

"I don't have to give you any reason. You are property. You may not question orders except to clarify your master's wishes."

A sigh escaped. "My knees and arms hurt." She wasn't about to tell him about her backside.

"Complaints are not permitted either."

"I'm sorry."

Blackthorn's quill on parchment was the only sound for a long while. Another growl from her stomach interrupted the silence. He stared at her.

"May I be allowed to know how long I must stay like this?"

"That is the first permissible question you have asked. The answer is 'no.' You will stay there as long as I see fit."

She swallowed hard and shifted her legs, maintaining the kneel. Tears slipped down her cheeks and she had no way to wipe or hide them.

"Why are you crying?" he demanded.

She sniffled, and then moaned her answer. "Because I hurt and I'm hungry and I don't understand what you want from me. And even if crying is forbidden, I can't help it."

"Crying isn't forbidden," he said with slightly less ice in his tone. He wrote more, looking back and forth between the parchment and her. Finally, he set the writing implements down. "The purpose of this session is to teach you that you are no longer free."

She nodded, resisting the urge to point out that she was acutely aware of that already.

"You do not need to know why an order is given. All you need to do is obey. You must not question your owner's right to lock you up. He has invested gold in you. You owe him unquestioning obedience. You're here to learn the proper attitudes toward your station."

"I understand."

"Excellent." He gathered his parchment and quill and headed for the door.

"If I have learned the lesson, won't you unlock my arms now? Please?"

"You must remember that I am always testing you, slave. Hold your tongue unless it's necessary."

"I'm sorry." The tears renewed their fervor, dropping silently and steadily.

He gave a frustrated sigh, then returned and crouched with the key, slipping it into the padlock. It clicked open and he removed it from her bands. She didn't move. He stood and circled her, showing her the padlock. Timmilina nodded in acknowledgement, but didn't move her arms.

"You may relax now," he said, sounding pleased.

She pulled her hands around and crossed them over her chest, pressing her fingers into sore arm muscles. Manacles clunked against her shoulder. Blackthorn reached toward her. She recoiled.

"I'm not going to hurt you," he whispered. He assisted her to her feet. Her legs wobbled with the uncertainty borne of numbness, but he steadied her. "There now. I promised you food, didn't I?"

"If I did well with training," she added sadly. Her guts wrenched with hunger she knew she'd have to endure.

"You did fine for a first day."

Did fine? Was she dreaming? She must have hit her head when Jonpur yanked her down. "I did fine?"

"I'm not allowed to reveal your scores, but you did well enough to eat." He ushered her to the table and into a chair.

Timmilina clenched her teeth to withstand the stinging needles of returning circulation. Blackthorn set a bowl of fruit down on the table, then returned attention to his notes. She grabbed a handful of berries and shoved them into her mouth.

"The duke is coming tomorrow. If you want to have any chance at catching his eye, I suggest that you use better manners than that. Or do you fancy Hannon Jonpur?"

"What does it matter?"

"I have to stay out of sales, but Duke Vahn has had a standing request for someone just like you for nearly a year now. I don't know if Jonpur would sell you, but if you're too stupid to see that you'd be better off with the duke, then you don't deserve to serve in his house."

"What do you mean, just like me?" she said around a mouth full of berries.

"A respectful Elva female who can lead his other house slaves with humility. The duke has the means to pay Jonpur double what he paid your father. Your father could have made much more if he had auctioned you."

Timmilina laughed so hard she nearly choked on berries. "Serves the bastard right," she muttered under her breath. Ruefully, she realized that she was the one cheated. She'd rather have her term reduced than have Gil make more gold.

"If the duke buys you, you'll have to learn third-person speech and strict protocols. His standards are very high and he pays us well to ensure we uphold them. But I've never known him not to give a slave a decent name—not majuscule or longer than two syllables, of course—but a name nevertheless. And he rarely hits his slaves."

"He doesn't punish?" she asked, tearing open an orange.

"Not all men are like your father and Jonpur. He wouldn't hit you for saying 'thank you'. His kind of punishment cleanses the soul."

That was just what she needed—someone who would justify beatings by passing it off as spirituality.

Blackthorn lowered his voice. "I shouldn't tell you this, but it's rumored that he doesn't exercise conjugal rights with his slaves. Perhaps he doesn't want to sully himself with Itzi. That's all he owns now. But you cannot refuse your owner, whoever he is."

Timmilina swallowed the pulp she'd barely chewed. No doubt, Jonpur would spend plenty of lust on her. Surprising he hadn't done it in front of Gil before dragging her off. All she could think about was survival, but this trainer wanted her to hope she still had a chance at marriage? Ridiculous! No one would want her in three years, used or not. Still, she couldn't shake Blackthorn's words. If she had to be ravaged, better by anyone than Jonpur. She didn't look up as she replied, "Do you really think the duke would buy me?"

"I wouldn't have brought it up if I didn't think so. But I have to remain neutral. Right now, Jonpur is the paying customer."

She nodded and scraped her teeth across the orange peel, sucking the last bit into her mouth. "Can you tell me how a slave should act in the presence of royalty?" she asked around the food.

He smiled. "Don't say anything unless he asks you directly. Keep your head bowed and hold your back straight. Other than that, don't do anything. Let him see you for a bargain, not a charity case."

She coughed at "bargain". Jonpur wouldn't part with his new toy cheaply, especially if some rich nobleman showed interest. Did she dare have any hope? She pushed the fruit bowl away. "Thank you for the food."

He didn't acknowledge her thanks. "He's due tomorrow near meridian toll. By that time, I'll have all your tests finished so you have a complete score. Let's get you down to the cells now. Training starts early."

He reattached the leash and led her to the slave quarters. They didn't reek of urine and excrement like she expected. Pungent citrus oil predominated instead. Stone halls echoed with weeping and moaning; none of the cells had doors. Each cell held four metal beds. Girls and women, the majority Itzi, were chained to the beds. Blackthorn stopped at an empty cell, locked her leash to a ring on the wall and her ankle to the bed frame.

She was so tired and the crude mattress so welcome that she didn't have time to wallow in self-pity or concentrate on her pain. Slumber rescued her. Others' cries and her own nightmares woke her several times, but sleep always came again.

Morning brought Blackthorn to unlock her from the bed and lead her on to more tests and lessons. Do this. Do that. Remember your place. Forget your will. Keep quiet. Kneel and grovel and answer questions. She did her best to comply, but she became more and more convinced she was failing. He didn't even believe her and forced her to drink a truth potion, then drilled her again.

Through it all, Blackthorn never struck her. He had to be holding back because of the anticipated sale—didn't want to damage the goods any more than they already were.

He left her alone in the training room while he went to meet Duke Vahn. She alternately paced the floor and sat on a wooden chair. Surely upholstered furniture wasn't for her use. Her trainer was gone at least a half an hour by her uncertain reckoning.

Blackthorn opened the door and announced, "His Royal Highness, Prince Vahn Rebono, duke of Latoph."

She knew she should kneel and bow, but she couldn't resist getting a look at him first.

A tall young man entered with a graceful and confident stride. He was dressed entirely in black—a silk poet's shirt, tailored jerkin, butter soft kidskin breeches, and polished boots. A silver and onyx tasseau fastened a velvet mantle that draped from his shoulders to the floor. He had a lean frame and an angular jaw line.

Timmilina caught herself before she ventured a look into his eyes. She slipped to her knees and bowed her head.

"This is the slave, your highness," Blackthorn said.

Gleaming black boots crossed the room. Timmilina clamped her jaw shut to keep her teeth from chattering. The boots stopped a few feet away. She closed her eyes and held her breath.

"Good afternoon," said a honey smooth voice.

"Good afternoon, your highness," she replied nervously.

"You may lift your head," the duke said.

Timmilina lifted her head, but not enough to look up to his face. It wasn't Blackthorn's earlier warnings that halted her. Even if she had met him as a freewoman, she didn't think she'd be venturing a look.

The duke gasped. "Why in Byntar…?"

"Oh, I forgot to warn you," Blackthorn explained hastily. "We didn't do that. Her father and owner did that yesterday—before she got here."

"But what did she do to warrant it?"

"It would be a breach of confidentiality for me to tell you, your highness. I have questioned her about it under truth potion and I do not believe her 'violations' would affect her service were she to belong to you."

"I see," he said thoughtfully. The duke extended his hand toward her face. She flinched. He withdrew. "What's your name?"

"Slave," she answered.

"No, I mean your given name."

"She is answering as her owner requires," Blackthorn said.

"Do you know who I am?" the duke asked.

"You are the king's son, the duke of Latoph, and the master of Rebono Keep."

"You are correct. And why should I purchase your contract?"

His choice of words touched her. Not 'why should I buy you,' but the contract. She shook her head. "I do not know that you should, your highness. Master said you might be interested, but I do not presume to know why."

75

"Your master knows of my interest?"

She furrowed her brows in frustration. "My trainer-master said that," she said, gesturing to Blackthorn. "I do not know what my owner-master knows. I have not seen him since yesterday."

"He does not know yet," Blackthorn added.

The duke strode away and motioned Blackthorn to join him. They stopped ten feet from her and lowered their voices, but she could still hear.

"I want her," the duke said.

"I thought you might," Blackthorn replied. Timmilina detected a chuckle in his voice. "That's why I sent for Hannon Jonpur."

Timmilina felt a chill course her spine at the mention of that name.

"What did he pay for her?" the duke asked.

"Three hundred gold. And her father signed off three years."

"That's barely enough for one year! Does he plan to auction her after training?"

"He intends to keep her himself."

"Then he may be resistant. Does he have any idea what she's really worth?"

"I am ethically bound to tell him her score. However, I am not obligated to mention that she's the highest scoring Elva we've had in ten years. And I never like to get into pricing."

"I owe you one."

"No, your highness. If you manage to buy this girl, I will be just as pleased as you."

The duke chuckled. "Thank you for showing her to me. You were right. She is just what I want as head of my house."

"Never let it be said that Galen Blackthorn can't spot an optimess for a good customer. I need a minute with Jonpur then I'll leave him for you. He's next door."

"Very pleasing."

Blackthorn slipped out the door and the duke returned to Timmilina. "When he returns, I'm going to negotiate with your owner. Unless you object?"

She shook her head. "No, your highness. If you would count me worthy to join your house, I would be honored. I swear that I will work hard for you." She wanted to add a promise never to attempt escape, but if he did too much "cleansing the soul", she didn't trust herself.

"That's about the best pledge a slave has ever made to me. If I manage to buy your contract, I'll be hard-pressed to match it."

Match it? What did that mean? They waited in silence.

"He's ready for you, your highness," Blackthorn said as he reentered.

"Do me a favor while I'm gone, Lord Blackthorn?"

"Of course, your highness."

"I want silver bands for her. High polish."

"Those have to be made to order and she can't wear them during training because there is no way to attach locks or chains. Ringed bands are required while she's here."

"Very well. At least procure some good steel ones then. That iron is hideous. Those come off the minute she's mine."

Blackthorn laughed. Timmilina wondered whether it was because the duke was so opinionated about the metal or because he was so sure he'd succeed. The duke left first, then Blackthorn spoke to her from the door, "Get off your knees a while. I'm going to hunt down some steel bands. Pray you get to wear them." The door clicked shut.

She stood and gazed out the barred window. In the distance, past the limestone buildings of the city, she could see the ocean. Had it been less than a day ago that she'd been there, agonizing over whether she owed her father any more care?

The duke returned before Blackthorn. He waved a key and a piece of parchment. "Got it," he said.

It had to be her contract. She smiled as widely as bruised cheeks allowed. "Thank you, your highness."

He slipped the key into her neck band. The lock clicked and the seam opened. As he removed it from her neck, he spoke in soft tones. "I'd like you to address me as 'Master Vahn', please."

"Thank you, Master Vahn," she revised. When the iron was removed, she marveled at the weight lifted.

He dropped the rusted collar to the floor with a thud and frowned at the abrasions on her neck. "You're welcome. Now for your name." He paused in his unlocking to scan the contract he'd set aside. "How about 'timna'?"

Society would call her foolish for being so pleased with a diminutive, but she was grateful to bear anything besides "slave". Beyond that, he'd taken the trouble to choose something close to her given name. "timna likes it very much, Master Vahn," she said. "Thank you."

"Blackthorn said you hadn't been trained in third person speech, the sly old fox." Manacles dropped to the floor next.

"I—I mean—timna hasn't yet. But he told m—timna that you favored it."

"I do indeed, and I'm pleased that you're trying already. That dreadful 'slave' moniker would never work. If I yelled 'slave!' in my house, four or five girls might trample each other trying to answer."

timna tittered a small laugh.

He lifted her chin. "I'm glad to see they didn't break you." She averted her gaze quickly. "Please look me in the eyes," he said.

Hesitantly, she peered up into his face. Never had she met a man so soft-spoken and gentle. His face was handsome, but betrayed his youth. His eyes were black, the pupil indistinct from the iris. While she wanted to explore the fathoms of his gaze, she couldn't bear him looking at her bruised face. Her cheeks heated with embarrassment, reminding her how much they still hurt.

"I always allow that once, so there's no curiosity," he explained.

"timna will never look again."

"Very pleasing. Now let's get those infernal irons off your ankles." He crouched with the key, unlocked the bands, and discarded them into the pile with the rest. "Much better."

"Thank you, Master Vahn."

"You're welcome. That's not permanent, but the new ones will not be so heavy."

"You are very kind," she said sheepishly.

"I'm glad you brought that—"

Blackthorn bustled in through the door. He blinked at them, his gaze darting between timna unfettered and the pile of rusty irons. "That was fast."

"I made him an offer he couldn't refuse," Master Vahn said with a tone that suggested that he'd used persuasions beyond gold.

"I don't doubt you did," Blackthorn chuckled. "Looks like I'm just in time with these." He offered the new hardware, pewter-colored and half the thickness of the iron.

Master Vahn shook his head. "Actually, if you could give me a room, I'd like to spend some time alone with her. I'll put the bands on when I'm done."

"Of course, your highness. Is this room acceptable?" Blackthorn's gaze lingered on the couch.

"Quite acceptable, thank you. Do you have a basin I could use?"

"There's one in the inhouse."

"Meet me back here in an hour then?"

"As you wish." Blackthorn set the bands on the table and slipped out.

"timna, would you please fill that basin and bring it to me?"

She was his slave, bands or not, and yet he still said please and asked rather than ordered. That earned him much in her estimation. "Yes, Master Vahn." She used the handpump to fill a glazed terracotta basin. She returned to him, carrying the water carefully.

In her absence, he'd taken a seat on the couch. He pointed to an end table. "Please set it there." She obeyed. He gestured to the floor at his feet; she caught his meaning and knelt where he'd indicated. Odd, but her backside didn't hurt so much this time. He removed a handkerchief from his jerkin and soaked it in the water. He wrung it, and then looked at her. "I'm going to touch your face now, all right?"

It wasn't a perfunctory question, not that he had to ask to begin with. He waited for her approval. "You don't have to do that," she whispered.

"I know I don't. I could have just as easily ordered you to do this yourself. But I elected to stay here with you for a reason. Can you guess why?"

It was rather obvious. He was seventeen and had just paid dearly for a virgin. She found it sweet how he wanted to wash her face and make her pretty first. However, with her bruises, it was an impractical goal. "Master wishes to deflower his virgin, yes?"

"De—deflower?"

"timna won't resist." Though still nervous, she meant it. He had rescued her from that abusive lout and she probably owed him her life. Besides, he was as gentle a man as she could ever hope to take that which she'd so foolishly saved.

He laughed. "I didn't buy you for that, timna. Although you are beautiful and I appreciate your submission, I'm married. I bought your contract, your service for the next three years—that's what I want from you."

Beautiful? Didn't intend to take her? She could hardly believe her ears.

"I don't believe in hitting females in the face, but I can't stand to see you wince every time I extend my hand to you. Trust is something that must be earned, so I asked for this time to start earning yours. I want you to get used to the idea that when I reach for your face, it's not a threat."

"Never?"

"Never. When one of my slaves commits an offense, I ask for her side of the story first and I let her know what the sentence is before I start. Discipline is never a surprise and never in the face."

timna's mind waged war over his words. He was so impossibly kind that it was difficult not to believe. Yet, she'd never met a man that didn't prattle sweet trifles, only to prove otherwise when mead or anger took over. Heavens, how she wanted to believe him. She nodded assent for him to touch her.

He pressed the kerchief to her face and wiped, taking care around the bruises. "When your training is over, you'll have a proper bath at home. This will have to suffice for now." Gently, he washed up to the hairline and down her neck, but stopped at the abrasions where the iron collar had been.

"Here," he said, offering the cloth. "You can finish now."

She accepted with a smile and resumed where he'd left off.

Before he leaned back, he tugged on her head cloth, and then pulled the pins from her bun. Long hair fell over her shoulders. He slid his hand down the length of it. "There. This is how I want you to wear it. No head cloth and no pins."

Only two classes of women wore their hair unbound in public—harlots who had no shame, and royalty, who were above it. She swallowed her pride and nodded.

"This is not a reflection of your character, timna. Anyone who dares question your virtue because of how I ask you to wear your hair will answer to my blade. I've defended my Itzi slaves for even less."

"You fight for the honor of slaves?" She regretted her audacity as soon as the question left her lips.

He didn't seem to mind. "Insults to my house are a direct affront to *me*. I do not tolerate slander."

She nodded lightly, still pondering all the ramifications of his words. He smoothed her hair with his fingers and she marveled to find it comforting.

"Until Lord Blackthorn returns, I have but one request of you, timna."

"Yes, Master Vahn?"

"Rest. Soon, you'll be in the throes of demanding training. Then you'll have to learn the rigors of Rebono Keep. It may be a long time before you have another chance like this."

She was half-convinced she was asleep already and this was but a dream. If she woke belonging to Jonpur again, she'd surely die. "That's all right. timna wasn't jesting about working hard for you."

She leaned against the side of the couch and rested as he'd ordained. He continued to stroke her hair, but neither spoke for a long interval.

He broke the silence. "The bands have to go back on now."

"Yes, Master Vahn." She hastened to the table where Blackthorn left the new bands. Picking them up, she gasped. "They're even lighter than they look!"

"The steel is specially made here. It is not what we use for swords or plowshares. The alloy is blended to be lightweight and rustproof."

"timna will remember not to attempt plowing with them."

He laughed. She knelt again and offered the bands first and then her wrists. He banded her with the new steel, first her wrists, then her neck, then her ankles. Compared to the bulky iron, she could hardly feel them.

He spoke as he locked them, using a formal tone. "These bands bind you to me, but they also bind me to you. In exchange for your obedience and service, I will provide shelter and sustenance. I promise to protect you as a member of my house and guard your honor."

Was this what he meant by "matching her pledge"? His words reverberated through her mind. If true, this young slavemaster would do more than Gil ever did. Nagging talons of past experience clawed at her psyche. She thought hard for several moments, staring at the last band he'd locked about her ankle. She lifted her head and found his hand outstretched, palm up.

Something that she hadn't felt since Mama died stirred deep within.

She placed her hand in his.

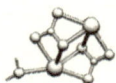

Gizile's hand went to her wrist. So entranced was she, that for a moment it seemed real. Rather than cold metal, she felt only warm flesh. After vigorously rubbing her wrists, she shivered from something more than the raw wind. What was happening to her? She looked up at her mentor, hoping for an answer. His jaw tightened, but he said nothing. He silently directed her attention back to the pool with an open hand. As the ice formed yet again, she found herself drawn to it. Unable to look away…unable to break free. The vision began. And Gizile became consumed.

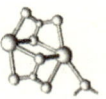

the kissing part

Fred Warren

A companion story to the novel *The Muse*

Stan Marino settled into his desk chair and switched on the computer. His epic fantasy novel, *Taron's Crusade*, was almost halfway finished, but he dreaded the next scene, a romantic interlude between his two main characters. These things were always tricky. He took a deep breath, flexed his fingers, and started typing.

Taron flipped a pebble into the water and watched it drift downward—ten, twenty, thirty feet. The Flower Pool was a miracle of sorts, heated by fires hidden deep within the bowels of the earth. The perfectly clear, blue water of the bell-shaped spring simmered with tiny, effervescent bubbles, even in mid-winter. It was one of his favorite places for contemplation, and he had much to consider this day.

Foliage rustled at the far end of the pool, and Taron's hand flashed to the dagger on his belt, relaxing as he saw the figure that emerged from the trees. It was an Elvish woman, tall and graceful, dressed in purple and gold, her long, silver hair bound at the nape of her neck with a shimmering jeweled clasp.

Siri. She raised a hand in greeting.

"Hi, Daddy!"

Stan pushed away from his desk and swiveled around to gather up his daughter. "Hannah! How's my girl?"

"Okay, I guess." She picked up a toy from Stan's cluttered desk, a windup monkey holding tiny brass cymbals, and fidgeted with it. "Mom told me not to bother you when you're writing, but I got bored."

"It's all right. I needed to take a break."

"Are you stuck again?"

Stan grimaced. "Maybe a little. This part of the story needs a woman's touch."

"I'm a woman. I could help."

"I don't know. It's grownup stuff."

"Please?" Hannah offered her best puppy-dog eyes, round and glistening.

Stan's heart melted. "Well, I guess you couldn't do any worse than me. Let's give it a shot."

"Hurray!"

She set the monkey back on the desk, its cymbals jingling in celebration. "You might have to read the story to me. Some of your words are comma-cated."

"Complicated?"

"That's what I said. Words I don't know yet."

"I think we can work around that. Here's what I've got so far. Taron is a king, and he's getting ready to lead a battle against some horrible goblins. He's sitting in his favorite thinking spot, and a beautiful lady steps out of the woods and waves at him."

Hannah's brow wrinkled. "Is she a princess?"

"Yes. She's a warrior princess. Her name is Siri, and her father rules the kingdom next door to Taron's. They've been friends for a long time."

"Are they sweethearts?"

Stan grinned. "Almost. I think they're going to get married at the end of the story."

"Is this the kissing part?"

"No...well, I don't know. It could be. I guess that's where you could help me. Do you think they should just talk like friends, or should they realize they're in love and share a kiss?"

"If there's a big battle coming up, I think they should get some kissing in while they have the chance."

"Fair enough. You can help me with Siri's part." Stan turned Hannah around in his lap so she faced the computer screen, and he reached around her to continue typing.

Taron scrambled through the brush bordering the pool, meeting Siri halfway around. They clasped hands.

"I'm glad you're here," he said. "There are so many things I need to tell you, so much I've left unsaid all these years."

"You could start by complimenting my hair," Siri replied, fluffing her silvery locks. "I got it fixed to make me 'specially gorgeous."

Stan paused and looked sharply at Hannah. "What?"

Hannah shrugged. "You think she's gonna kiss him if he doesn't say something nice about her hair? Mom's right—you don't understand women at all."

"Now, hold on a minute!"

"I'm just trying to help."

"Okay, okay. We'll do it your way."

Hannah nodded primly. "Thank you."

"Oh, Siri, it's been so long since I've seen you like this, when war was only a distant smudge on the horizon. You're beautiful. Your hair shines like liquid moonlight—I've always admired it. I'm sorry I've never told you before."

"It's about time. Do you like my dress? It's real expensive, but I'm worth it."

"Hannah Marie…"

"I can go back upstairs if you want."

"No, let's keep writing. I'm curious about where this is going."

Taron lifted one hand over Siri's head and turned her around. "This is a lovely gown. It compliments your eyes perfectly."

"Thank you. My shining blue eyes are one of my coolest features. Everybody says so."

Taron pulled her close to him. "You've been my friend and comrade-in-arms for so long, I never stopped to consider my true feelings for you. I love you, Siri. I've been a blind fool, but I'm certain now that whatever the future holds, we must face it together."

She was so lovely. Her eyes held him in thrall, deeper and warmer than the aquamarine waters of the Flower Pool. Taron lifted her head to press his lips to hers.

Siri turned her face away. "What kind of girl do you think I am? I don't kiss boys on the first date. You have to take me out to dinner, and a movie, and maybe bowling. Then we smooch."

"Hold on. I thought you said they need to hurry up and kiss before the battle starts."

"I changed my mind. It's a woman's purr-dog-a-tive."

"Prerogative."

"Whatever."

"Oy. All right. Let's try this…"

Taron hesitated. He was moving much too quickly. His love for Siri was strong, but leaping from friendship to passion wasn't fair to her. The war was so close at hand, a war they might not survive.

Siri looked up at him. "My neck is getting stiff. Either kiss me now, or take me bowling. Make up your mind."

Gentle breezes wafted a musical voice through the forest. "Come on, you two! Your dinner's getting cold."

Siri groaned. "My mother's calling. We have to go."

Stan lifted Hannah from his lap and set her on her feet. She trotted upstairs. "Thanks, Hot Dog," he called after her, "that's the most fun writing I've had in a long time."

"You're welcome."

Stan looked at the passage they'd written together, and he smiled. He couldn't keep this in the story, but it was priceless all the same. With a couple of mouse clicks, he saved the file. It might come in handy at her wedding reception.

Warm arms encircled his neck. Stan's wife, Charity, peered over his shoulder at the page on the screen, chuckling as she read. "What's this all about?"

"Hannah was helping me with my story. She shows real promise as a writer, but her approach to romance is…unusual. We may want to warn her first boyfriend."

Charity smiled. "There's time enough for that. I think this scene is missing something, though."

"What's that?"

She maneuvered herself into Stan's lap and rubbed noses with him. "You left out the kissing part."

"Would you like to help me take care of that?"

"Yes, but you'll have to say something nice about my hair first. What kind of girl do you think I am?"

Gizile touched the nape of her neck and felt the shortness of her hair, then looked down at the brown of her robe and the bright red of her cloak that warned she was still merely a student. The sudden ache in her heart surprised her. There was so much love in that vision, as there had been a different sort of love in the vision before. What she wouldn't give to live in that world. What would become of her once her studies were complete? Would she marry? Would any man have an orphan? She stole a look at Tok's grim countenance; was that a gleam of amusement in his eye?

"Child, you worry so much about the future. Your worries steal your laughter, your joy. Accept yourself for who you are."

She looked back at the pool, telling herself that something must be wrong with her. She was nothing special. Right?

The wave crashed and the ice formed. A little girl looked at her…a little girl who appeared as dejected as Gizile felt.

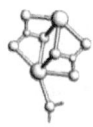

the artist

Kat Heckenbach

A companion story to the novel *Finding Angel*

I was six when I began to understand what the whispering was all about. My parents did their best to pretend everything was fine, that I wasn't different from the rest of them. But children are amazingly aware of their surroundings, and I had an especially keen eye for detail. Unfortunately, an eye for detail isn't magical.

"It's got to show up some day," my dad said, not bothering to keep his voice down. My parents thought I was playing in the back yard as I crouched behind the hedges below the open window.

"Caryn's nearly seven now, Roger. Her Talent should have shown up years ago." I heard my mother sniff. "Maybe we should take her to the doctor."

"No! There's nothing wrong with her." A thump like a fist hitting a wooden tabletop. "She can already do magic like everyone else. Her Talent will develop in its own time. We just have to be patient."

I scooted to the end of the hedge and dashed across the back yard to my tree house. After I climbed inside, I crumpled to the floor and cried. My Talent was never going to show up. I would never have anything more than ordinary magic. It wasn't fair! Everyone had something they could do better than the rest—why not me?

My father would say, "Magic comes in bits and pieces, Caryn. And the biggest piece is always last." But I'd known better. My cousin had shown signs of his Talent when he was only six months old. Most of my neighborhood friends were at least showing the beginning stages, like William Kleidon who carved magical wood and changed it to stone without losing the wood's powers.

I wiped the tears from my cheeks with the back of my hand and took a deep breath. My eyes felt puffy, and I didn't want my parents knowing I'd been crying, so I stayed in the tree house for a while, drawing. Even at six I showed real skill, but an eye for detail isn't magical, nor is being able to draw well.

By the time I turned eight I'd given up. My Talent would never develop. At least I had my art. I spent every spare moment drawing or painting. It was a release for me, a compulsion. My walls were covered with sketches of plants and animals from the forest. I gave them away to friends and family, and even sold a few in town. Everyone oohed and ahhed over my ability to capture the colors. They said my paintings "popped off the page." But the praise was always followed by a look of pity.

Around strangers I pretended I was one of those people who liked to keep their Talents secret. I even began to wonder if some of them were pretending, too.

"Don't be silly," William said one day as we walked through the forest looking for fallen branches. At ten, he stood a full head taller than me even though his birthday was six months after mine. "It's just that some people have really weird Talents, or they don't see the value of them, so they keep quiet. But we've all been given gifts, Caryn." He stopped and looked at me with those bright blue eyes so full of friendship and concern. "Yours is in there somewhere. You just haven't figured out how to reach in and pull it out."

My cheeks warmed and I turned away. Why did he have to be so sweet? I didn't deserve a friend like him, someone whose Talent outshone everyone else's as far as I was concerned. He had gone beyond turning wood into stone, and could now transform any natural substance into any other. I was jealous and proud of him at the same time.

The flush left my cheeks when I spied a branch half-hidden behind a toadstool. I reached down and grabbed it, and then held it out for William to see.

"This one would be perfect, don't you think? It looks like Water Maple, and it's big enough around, isn't it?"

William's face widened with a smile that crinkled his eyes. "Yes! If I carve it into a sphere, I can hollow out the middle and transform it to crystal."

"That's what I was thinking," I said, as the flush returned, but on my neck now instead of my cheeks. Sometimes it seemed as if he read my thoughts.

We spoke at the same time then—"A snow globe!"—and William grabbed my hand as we ran to his house.

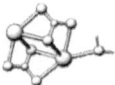

The snow globe sat in a place of honor on my nightstand. The dragon figurine William had put inside it was such a deep purple it appeared black. Until the sun hit it just right, then it burst into iridescent swirls.

I picked up the globe and shook it, then leaned in and watched the tiny flakes settle.

"I'll be thirteen tomorrow," I said to the dragon. "Almost a woman." My throat closed up and I buried my face in my pillow. A woman with no Talent.

My sobbing had barely subsided when my mom stepped into the room.

"Honey," she said as she laid her hand on my back, "William's here."

"Tell him I'll be right out." My voice croaked, and my mom squeezed my shoulder.

"Take your time, sweetie. We'll be downstairs when you're ready."

I listened to her soft footsteps as she left my room, and then sat up. *Get a grip, Caryn.* Who needed a Talent when I had Mom and Dad? And…William. My gaze fell on my latest painting. It hung over my dresser and nearly filled the wall. Being an artist would have to do. Not a magical Talent, but talent nonetheless. The corners of my mouth quivered, but I managed a smile and headed downstairs.

My mood lifted when I saw William. He held out a huge, wrapped package, but I ran past it and threw my arms around his neck.

"Whoa," he said, returning the hug, and then stepped back. His smile crinkled his eyes as always, and my neck grew warm. "Come on, I can't wait another second for you to open your present."

I laughed as I ripped the paper, and then gasped when I saw what he'd made for me. The picture frame looked like no wood I'd ever seen before. Different grains and shades of brown swirled together as though made from liquid.

William cleared his throat, and looked down. "I, um, Transformed several different kinds of wood into oil, poured it into a mold, and Transformed them back again. I had no idea if it'd even work, but…"

"It's beautiful!" I cried. "And I know just the picture I want to hang in it." I grabbed his hand and led him up to my room. He laid the frame on my bed while I pulled out my largest sketchbook.

"This is the one."

I watched him scrutinize the drawing.

"That's the lily we saw in the forest. I can't believe you drew that from memory. It looks totally real."

"Well, I had no choice." Butterflies flitted around in my stomach and I tried to hide how nervous his gaze made me. I walked over and laid the picture in the middle of the frame. "I could never pick one from the forest. They're too rare. But I've always wanted one." I adjusted the paper, and looked closely at my drawing.

I squinted. *What is that?*

"There's a smudge," I said, reaching toward the paper. When my hand brushed the picture, my palm tingled and I pulled back. My eyes widened and my ribcage tightened around my lungs.

"What's wrong," William said. He sounded distant. The room tilted.

"N-nothing."

I reached back down and touched the picture again with the tips of my fingers, and the tingling traveled up to my wrist. I forced air into my lungs and pushed against the paper. There was no resistance. I inched my hand forward until I felt the silky softness of flower petals. It took all my strength to hold my hand in place. I trembled from head to foot.

"Keep going," William whispered from over my shoulder. The sound of his voice calmed my trembling.

My hand seemed to move forward on its own, as if obeying William's mind and not mine. I held my breath as my fingers wrapped around the lily.

When I pulled my hand from the picture, the lily remained in my grasp.

"Happy Birthday, Caryn," William said. He grabbed my shoulders and turned me to face him. His eyes held all the sunshine in the world, and his smile made me tremble all over again even as he cupped my hands with his. "I told you, didn't I? That someday you'd figure out how to pull your Talent out."

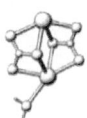

Gizile's heart drummed in her chest. She rubbed the ring on her left finger with the tip of her thumb. Could she actually learn to use it? Could she follow in her mother's footsteps after all? Maybe she wasn't really a failure. Perhaps she would find love as well.

Maybe she just needed more time. She felt the ring warm as the power began to awaken, for the first time beyond the mere tingle of activation. She held her breath, feeling the warmth engulf her hand.

"Don't summon the power 'til you have need of it, girl." Tok's sepulcher-toned voice was quiet and unsurprised.

"But I've never before—"

"Just because you can...doesn't mean you should."

She quickly opened her hand, the cold returning as the power waned. Another wave had washed in. She leaned closer, wondering what the crystalline ice would show her next. An older lady appeared that reminded Gizile of her own grannie. And a young boy who could have been her brother. She leaned closer. Could it be? Surely not...

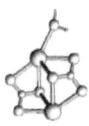

a stretch of time

Grace Bridges

"Kuia, how come you've always got more time than anyone else?"

I smiled. My youngest mokopuna was entering the age of reason. "You wanna know why, boy? I'm retired."

Rawiri screwed up his face. "No, Kuia, not that. The real reason. How you wrote all those books before you retired."

"Yes, there were many things to do, and I did them all."

"Did you write them at work?"

I frowned. "No! That's a wrong thing to do, son of my son. I worked a full day."

"Well then, how'd ya do it? I know you're fast. I see you walk into the kitchen and next minute you're telling us the grub's up."

We both looked up as Rawiri's mother poked her head out the porch door. "I'm just here for a minute—have to go and sort out your sister's netball uniform. Will you be all right with your Nan a bit longer, Rawiri?" She shot a pleading glance at me, and I smiled at her. She sighed. "When I'm finished I'll come sit with you for a bit too, Kuia. I need some of that peacefulness of yours."

She vanished, and we heard her run through the house and out to the car before driving away.

I turned my attention back to the boy. "If I tell you how I did all these things without rushing, will you promise to keep it secret? Just between you and me?"

Rawiri's eyes grew wide. "Aw, yeah!"

"All right. Listen to this story…"

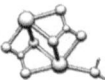

Once upon a time there was a young girl, and as you have rightly guessed, that young girl was me. She juggled her job and her husband and children, and tried to find still more time for things she liked to do, such as reading books and telling stories. But there were never enough hours in the day. Night after night she fell asleep exhausted, without accomplishing any of the things she wanted to. There was only time for what must be done, and nothing extra.

My kuia observed all this for a while, and heard my complaining. Now this kuia was a very wise kaimatua, an elder among the people. She took me aside one day to speak to her. I brought her a mug of coffee and we sat in the creaky swing chair on the back porch, looking out over the tangled bush at the bottom of the section.

"Moko, you cannot go on like this. The great god Io gives the same twenty-four hours to each one of us. He must think it is sufficient, so why is it too little for us?"

"But Kuia, when Io created the world there was no thought of modern life. Nowadays we have many more demands on our time."

"Would you have Io extend the length of each day? Would you have him place extra hours in it?"

"I would. And surely he can." I controlled my frustration with an effort.

Kuia's jaw dropped just a little, but her eyes took on an even deeper tinge, if that were possible. "Such faith in a young one. Yet to them that believe, nothing shall be impossible." She took a careful sip of her coffee and made a face. "Bah. Too hot."

I looked up into her beloved, wrinkled face. "Mother of my mother, what is this you say? Io is willing to stretch the hours of my days?"

"Are you willing to receive the gift?"

"You play games with me, old woman."

"Riddles, maybe, but never games."

I struggled with myself, for I did not want to appear silly if indeed she was joking with me. But I was still a child at heart, and curious to match. What did it matter if my pride should take a tumble?

She caught my eye as I looked up, and I let a smile curl my lips. "All right, Kuia, I am willing. What is this gift?"

"Ka pai, little one. Now listen." She closed her eyes, raised a hand, and let forth a stream of Maori which I did not wholly understand, though I picked up words like *gift* and *time* and *spirit*. In essence, she was bestowing a spiritual gift of time upon me.

If it was real, that is. I blinked myself to attention.

"There," said Kuia, "that's it."

Something flashed by, so quick it was at the edge of my vision before it registered. The whole world turned purple for an instant. I caught myself thinking something really happened, and shook my head to clear it.

"Just what is 'it'? How does it work?"

Kuia laughed. "I don't know, hon. That's the mystery the Good Lord's keeping to himself. Maybe you'll figure it out and let me know."

I gave her an unconvinced smile and was about to turn away. There were things to do, after all.

But she caught my arm. "One thing. It only works when no one's looking. When you're alone."

I nodded and went about my chores. I cleaned up the children's lunch mess—dishes, table and floor. I dried the dishes and put them away, then glanced at the clock over the mantelpiece. My hand reached to shake it. I'd only just changed the battery.

Turning, I sought the window and was relieved to see Kuia's head and shoulders where she sat on the porch. She held the coffee mug, unmoving.

Wait. Was that…a wisp of steam? Hanging in the air above the mug?

I shook my head and went to get the vacuum cleaner and carried it upstairs to begin the weekly round.

Much later, I finished and put the machine away, then jammed my fists in the small of my back and stretched my aching muscles. I walked with slow paces through the kitchen, not looking at the clock, to the laundry and dragged a load of wet washing into the basket. I heaved it outside and down to the line near the porch. I turned to peg up the heavy sheets and covers, and caught Kuia staring at me.

But she didn't say anything, so I finished quickly and went back inside.

Funny. The clock hand had moved a couple of minutes. I looked at the door, then back at the clock. Well, I'd take the clock apart later maybe. Right now there was work to do. I was lucky the baby was still sleeping.

So I ran a scrubbing brush over the bathroomware and dried it off again, then got the mop and bucket out and washed the downstairs floors. By now I was about ready to drop, but everything was done and the baby was still quiet. I tiptoed into his room and watched his sleeping angel face for a while. I didn't know what time it was because of that silly clock not working, but it felt late in the day. The older kids would soon return from school and fill the house with their chatter and play.

But the little one—your father, Rawiri—slept on in his bliss, so I slipped out again to get myself a coffee. I was about to pour away the last batch and make a new one, but then I realised it was still steaming, and I hadn't left the element on.

I whirled and caught the clock in both hands. It had moved maybe eight minutes since I'd first come in from talking to Kuia. That's how long I'd have taken to hang up the sheets and check on the baby. *Only when you're alone?*

I rushed outside to the porch, where Kuia sat exactly as I'd left her. Steam still rose from her coffee mug, and she hadn't been inside for a refill.

She peered around at me, a twinkle in her eye. "You got something done, then?"

"I—I did!" Gulp. "How long did that take me?"

"Not quite ten minutes. Coffee's just right now, babe."

So the clock wasn't wrong? "There's still hours till the kids come home from school!"

"Why not take a nap?"

My mind raced with the consequences. Overnight I'd not be alone, so I couldn't make up for the extra hours then. I'd have to take a snooze during the day, and hope the gift of time extended to sleep.

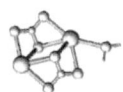

"It did, right?" Rawiri leaned forward, eyes bright. "Cause you never nap for very long."

"You have seen the truth of it, boy." I leaned back in the wicker chair and closed my eyes.

Some time later I was woken by a touch on my arm and the smell of coffee. Rawiri pushed the mug into my hands and sat down on the step. "So are you able to pass on this gift as well?"

My, the child was onto it. "I've never tried. But just in case I would need to, I learned our people's language."

"Won't it work in English?"

"I thought it best to cover all the possibilities. I had plenty of time, after all."

Rawiri nodded, then scrambled to his feet. "I have plenty of time too, Kuia. When I am old enough to run out of it sometimes, I will ask you for this gift." He ran off down the garden and vanished between the trees.

I blinked. He was wiser than his years. But when the time came, I would pray the words over my grandson and he would bear the gift of time for the next generation.

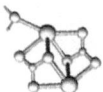

Gizile thought of her own two grannies. For Gizile's sake, they observed an undeclared armed truce so as to teach her the things grannies teach—the only time of peace between them. Thinking of them brought her mind to her parents. Her heart ached. Fire and ice, drawn together only over her. If only she could have stretched time while they were here…

Time! She looked at the length of her shadow on the beach. To turn and look at the location of the afternoon sun would draw a sharp rebuke from Tok. She guessed two hours more before sunset. Her eyes returned for the approaching wave.

A classroom formed, and Gizile smiled. Students. Like her.

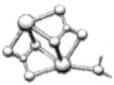

one smile at a time

Fred Warren

The air-conditioning is broken again. Even with the windows open, the classroom is hot, relentless Southern humidity lending an unwelcome heaviness to the air. The children labor on at their exercises without complaint, the murmur of calculations masking the drone of a red-legged wasp blundering its way among the light fixtures. My students are accustomed to the heat, though the more timid among them would be mightily distracted by the wasp.

I walk between the neat rows of desks, offering encouragement here, a gentle correction there, a firm tap on a drowsy shoulder toward the back of the room. A furtive memory tiptoes through an idle corner of my mind…iced lemonade and cool ocean breezes. I hear the cheerful clamor of the second-graders charging onto the playground outside, and the memory strengthens, perhaps emboldened by their call to twenty minutes of liberty and anarchy.

A few heads turn longingly toward the sound for a moment, but they know better than to linger. Their turn will come, but only if their assignments are finished on time. I move toward the window, watching children leap onto the swings, slides, and sundry other bits of weather-worn equipment in a chaotic scramble of arms and legs. The lemonade tastes sweeter, the breezes grow cooler, and I remember Penny.

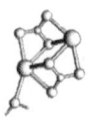

Fifteen years ago, a naïve kid fresh out of college, I came to this sleepy little town ready to change the world.

It wasn't much to look at then. A bank, Woolworth's, Standard Oil station (full service), mom-and-pop grocery, two stoplights, a fabric mill, and half a dozen churches of various flavors.

Three thousand people, give or take a dozen. About two-thirds white, Scottish-Irish stock, mostly. One-third black. A handful of more recent immigrants pretty much kept to themselves. A couple of Cuban families relocated from Florida, a small clan of Hmong, a few Chinese. Old Chen Lee ran a little take-out restaurant on Forest Avenue favored by the State Troopers.

The turmoil of the sixties was still remembered, but fading, and folks were largely civil to one another, though the railroad tracks that bisected the town reflected a quiet segregation that persisted in its private affairs. An old scar that itched every once in a while, just to let you know it was still there. Us on this side, you on that side, everyone minds their own business, and we all get by.

I applied for and was accepted to fill a third-grade teaching position at Tubman Elementary, unofficially known as "the black school," though a few of the poorer white families zoned for it who couldn't afford private school sent their children there. I was a novelty. They'd never had a white man on the faculty. Certainly they'd never had a man teaching third-graders.

The other teachers were wary at first, though as the days wore on, the shared tribulations of teaching young children broke down most barriers. People smiled, commiserated, and offered to share a table at lunch. There was still a reserve, though, an invisible boundary that couldn't be crossed. This far, but no farther. I like you, but there are some things you can never understand, some things we can't discuss. It stung a little. I'd grown up believing that no differences were insurmountable, if your heart was pure and you reached out in honest friendship.

The children, however, were wonderful from the beginning, their acceptance of me, once they'd overcome the awkwardness of this strange anomaly in their classroom, complete. They studied hard, and they followed directions. I was having a wonderful time at my chosen vocation. Life was good—suspiciously good.

I said as much at lunchtime one day, and my companions at the table smiled and nodded knowingly at one another.

"Boy's a little slow on the uptake."

"Now, you be sweet to Mister Joseph. This is his first year teaching. How's he supposed to know?"

"You lucked out, son."

I was mystified at this reaction. "Okay, I'll bite. What's going on?"

"You got a little girl in your class, name of Penny Williams?"

"There's a Penelope Williams. She's a fine student."

More rocking back in chairs and smiling. "Mmm-hmm. Told you so."

"Told me what?"

"That gal's a genuine good-luck charm. When she's around, things just go *right*. Kids behave themselves, lessons go according to plan, heck, sometimes even the air seems cooler when she's around."

"Not just in school, neither. Her daddy's pastor at the AME church. Congregation's doubled over the last two years. Never been vandalized in all that time. Children in her Sunday School class aren't ever absent, unless the family goes out of town. By the way, when's the last time you had a child miss class, Mister Joseph?"

Frankly, I couldn't remember the last time I'd had an absence, or even a tardy, but the conversation was so patently ridiculous, I wasn't about to admit that and contribute to the prevailing lunacy. "I don't believe this," I blustered. "Here we are, educated people, and we're talking about magic charms. One of my students is some kind of human rabbit's foot?"

"Not rabbit's foot…Lucky Penny. Seeing is believing, young man. Watch her closely for a while. You'll see."

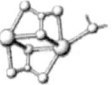

So, against my better judgment, I watched Penelope Williams a little more carefully. Her behavior was extraordinary only in its consistency. Miss Williams was always well-behaved, always studious, and always cooperative with her classmates. Her diet was unremarkable. She ate the cafeteria food without complaint, even if she never seemed to find enough time to finish her lima beans or Brussels sprouts. It would have been suspicious if she had. On the playground, she favored jump rope and tetherball, though she was content to simply stroll about the yard, smiling a quiet little Mona Lisa smile, waving here and there at her friends, laughing at some shouted joke or whispered confidence.

If there was anything magical about Penny Williams, I wasn't seeing it. She was a nice little girl, and perhaps that was magic enough. I felt like some backwater cop on a stakeout, waiting through endless hours of stale donuts and cold cups of coffee for something, anything, to happen. Dull, dogged flatfoot that I was, I kept watching.

Nothing interesting transpired until Penny's family took a trip over two school days in the middle of October. Was it just my imagination, or was the class a little harder to handle, a little more fractious than usual, a little less focused on their lessons?

Maybe it was the heat. The cooler wasn't working, and opening the windows didn't generate enough flow to clear the stuffy air from my classroom. I couldn't blame the confluence of Indian summer and a seized compressor on the absent mystical aura of a nine-year-old pixie from south Alabama, could I? My colleagues passed me in the hallway with Cheshire Cat grins, sage nods, or amusedly tolerant shakes of the head and the ever-inscrutable "Mmm-hmm."

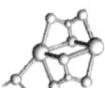

It took literally a change in perspective to break my stubborn disbelief in the Lucky Penny. One blustery November afternoon, amid a long haul of inserting commas and correcting misspellings in red ink, I leaned back in my chair and refocused my bleary eyes on the view through the classroom window, the one overlooking the playground. In mid-stretch, I froze.

A hurricane was moving slowly across the yard. I blinked a few times, rubbed my eyes, and looked again.

Well, it wasn't exactly a storm, or it was a peculiarly benign one. It swirled across the pavement and gym equipment, over and among the random clusterings of jumping, running, and squabbling children, pulling the disorder of their movements into a whirling moiré pattern, like iron filings drawn together along the lines of a magnetic field. Fights dissolved, motion harmonized, and bouncing balls, thudding feet, and childish chatter knitted into a syncopated thrum of sound, like a beehive, as the invisible vortex drew more children into itself.

At the heart of the un-storm was Penny Williams, smiling, nodding, laughing, and waving, as if it were the most ordinary thing in the world to be the eye of a benevolent human cyclone meandering about the playground of Harriet Tubman Elementary.

I stared, dumbfounded, for some indeterminate period of time, until Penny happened to glance upward…and must have seen me staring at her through the window, mouth agape.

She regarded me uncertainly for a moment, then her face lit up with an incandescent smile. A warm breeze seemed to wash over me, tangy with salt and citrus, comforting and familiar. My grandparents' backyard in Monterrey…I sipped lemonade while we watched an orange beach-ball sun sink slowly into the ocean. The memory was so strong, it was nearly tangible.

Penny waved merrily and skipped off in a new direction, order and harmony spinning along in her wake.

I asked her to stay for a few moments after the last bell. "Penny," I asked, "what happened out there on the playground this afternoon?"

"Just playin', Mister Joseph. Enjoyin' the day. It was a fine day to be outside, don't you think?"

"Yes, I suppose it was. Quite a wonderful day. You're a bit of a wonder yourself, Penny. Things seem to go better when you're around. Has anyone ever told you that?"

She grinned. "Oh, sure. Mama says people just naturally like me. Miz Watkins at church told me I've got the gift of helps. She said that means God uses me to give people exactly what they need, when they need it. Daddy says I should just be a good girl and not get any uppity notions in my head."

"That sounds like pretty good advice. What do *you* think?"

"I think I want to make people happy. They're so sad most of the time. If I can do something to help people be happier, then I should do it, shouldn't I, Mister Joseph?"

I couldn't argue with that logic. No matter the source of her mysterious influence, it didn't seem to be harmful. "Of course you should, Penny," I replied. "Better hurry along now. Your folks will be happier if you're home on time."

For several days afterward, I wrestled with my discovery. Perhaps it would be better to simply go on as if nothing extraordinary had happened. Everyone seemed to be aware that there was something special about Penny Williams, but it wasn't any more unsettling to them than the turn of the seasons, or gravity.

But what of the possibilities? What was the extent of Penny's ability? Did she use it consciously? Could she be trained to focus it for a specific purpose? Was it a skill that others could learn to employ? I imagined a hundred or so Pennys traveling around the world, ushering in the Peaceable Kingdom with pineapple-scented tropical breezes, and the vision was irresistible.

Penny was right—if I could do something to make the world happier, I should do it. I'd need to speak with her parents.

The First African Methodist Episcopal Church was an unassuming red-brick building one block north of Main Street, passed to the AME congregation when the United Methodists upgraded to a larger house of worship at the edge of town. There was no answer when I knocked at the parsonage next door, so I tried the main entrance to the sanctuary. The door was unlocked, and I could hear the whine of a vacuum cleaner inside the building.

The interior was simply furnished and well-tended. There were two rows of oak pews, glistening with a fresh rubbing of lemon oil, the odor lingering pleasantly in the air. A low platform at the front held a small lectern, four folding chairs, and a set of three-tiered risers, presumably for the choir, with a large wooden cross on the back wall and two doors to either side.

A stout black lady in a flowered dress and lacy white headscarf switched off the vacuum cleaner, and inspected me quizzically. "May I help you?"

"I'm Darrin Joseph," I said. "I teach at Tubman Elementary. Is Reverend Williams here today?"

She frowned. "*Pastor* Williams is in his study. Take the door on the left, young man, last room on the right at the end of the hallway."

"Thank you."

"If the door's closed, Pastor's workin' on his sermon, so don't knock 'less it's an emergency, understand?"

"Yes, ma'am."

The woman smiled, nodded, and resumed her vacuuming.

I found the pastor's office easily enough, but the door was ajar, not quite open or closed, so I knocked tentatively.

"Door's open, come on in." Pastor Williams smiled and rose to shake my hand as I entered. He was an imposing man, with a grip like steel. "It's good to see you again, Mister Joseph. I enjoyed your presentation at Parents' Night. Have a seat. Everything going well at school?"

"Yes, sir. Some of the kids are struggling with math this quarter, but they'll have it sorted out by report card time."

"And how's Penelope doing? Working hard, I hope. Behaving herself?"

"Always. Penny's one of my best students. She's a joy to teach. In fact, that's why I'm here. I needed to talk with you about Penny…and her future." I spent the next several minutes describing Penny's uncanny effect on people around her and its potential applications.

Pastor Williams listened without interrupting. His silence continued for a few moments after I finished, then he sighed. "Do you think you're the first person to suggest my daughter has some strange power that must be harnessed for the good of mankind?"

"Well, no, I just thought…"

"No, you didn't think at all," he said. "I've had to relocate my family twice since Penny turned five years old. Her kindergarten teacher came to me with a story like yours. She suggested we send Penny to a research institute for evaluation. When we rejected her proposal, she called Social Services, claiming we were neglecting Penny. It was only through the grace of God and a sympathetic judge that our daughter wasn't taken from us.

"We moved to a different state, but one of the deacons in our church there took it into his head that Penny was possessed of a familiar spirit. He called the Bishop and demanded we exorcise her. The Bishop supported me, but the deacon carried a great deal of influence in the local community, so we had to move again.

"This congregation loves Penny, and she's happy here. I will not uproot my family again, nor will I subject my daughter to scientific analysis because some well-meaning person is convinced they know what's best for her. Do you understand me?"

"Yes, sir. I'm sorry. I had no idea."

The angry tone softened a little. "Just leave it alone. My daughter likes you, Mister Joseph, and by all accounts, you're a fine teacher. Please restrict your efforts on behalf of Penny to her education. If she is doing well in school, we have nothing further to discuss. Good day."

So that was that. I kicked myself for becoming so caught up in my vain imagination that I'd alienated a parent and nearly sent a little girl back into a nightmare she'd survived twice already.

I abandoned the detective game and focused on schoolwork. Fall turned into winter, and the children struggled through math, most emerging triumphantly with good marks going into Christmas vacation.

It was a pleasant time, and ordinary enough, though I noticed a change in the air from cool seas and citrus to warm gingerbread and pine whenever Penny was nearby.

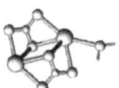

Spring was tardy that year. Icy winds still lashed at the windows in mid-March. The fabric mill laid off a quarter of its work force, and many of the children came to school each day with eyes mirroring their parents' fear and stress.

When she wasn't working on her assignments, Penny flitted around my classroom like a pigtailed hummingbird, wordlessly dispensing encouragement and hope, gently filling the air with the aroma of new flowers and the whisper of birdsong, just at the edge of perception. The effort of raising everyone's spirits against so much despair must have worn on her, and she seemed tired at day's end, while the rest of us returned home refreshed from our stay in Penny's little oasis.

I stopped her one day as she was packing up her books. "Thank you, Penny," I said. "I know what you're trying to do, and how hard it must be. You're helping a lot of people get through a difficult time."

She sighed. "I can't keep it to myself. Daddy wishes I would, but when I see somebody hurting, I want to take some of the hurt away. It's not just in school. There's lots of people hurting, and I want to help them all, but there are so many, and I'm just me."

"Well, there's a lot of power in just being you. Don't worry about saving the whole world. Just try to make it a better place, one smile at a time."

"Saving the world one smile at a time." Her eyes regained their sparkle. "I like that."

"I suppose I'm trying to improve the world myself, one math problem at a time, but I think your way is more fun."

We both laughed. It would be a long time before I laughed again.

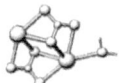

On March 31st, the man with the gun came to Tubman Elementary. His name was Bill Stevens, and he'd been pink-slipped in the fabric mill layoff.

After two weeks in the bottle, he staggered to our school with a loaded pistol, looking for his foreman's son. He shot the security guard and two teachers on his way in, then put a bullet in my shoulder as I tried to stop him from pushing through the door into my classroom. Some of the children screamed as I went down, most dived under tables and desks. A few just stood frozen, jaws slack, tears running down their cheeks.

"Shut up!" Stevens roared. "I want Joey West! Where is he?"

Joey was curled up in a ball at the back of the room, and I prayed he was too terrified to respond. I could feel blood pooling beneath me, and every movement was agony as I tried to keep both the gunman and my students in view.

Then I saw Penny. She crouched under her desk, her face tear-stained but set in determination, not fear.

She locked eyes with me, and though her lips were quivering, she managed a smile. A gentle breath of air mingled with jasmine and chocolate wafted over me, and I knew what she was planning.

"No, Penny!" I hissed. "Stay down!"

Stevens began stumbling around the room, turning over desks. "Where are you, Joey?" he crooned. "I'm gonna make your old man sorry. Tossed me out like a piece of garbage. That job was all I had. Time for him to know what it feels like to lose everything."

Penny stood up. "Please don't hurt anybody else, mister."

Stevens turned, looked Penny up and down dazedly. "You ain't Joey West. Where's Joey?"

Penny turned on her million-watt smile. "Put the gun down. You don't need to hurt anybody. You just want...you want..." The smile faltered. Something was very wrong.

"What're you doing?" Stevens shook his head, as if trying to regain his equilibrium. "Stop it! Get outta my head!" He lifted the gun, his hand shaking.

Penny's determination vanished. She backed away from Stevens, her face a mask of shock and panic. "No, please. Don't," she whimpered.

I struggled to get my feet underneath me, to put myself between Penny and this lunatic, but a wave of pain surged through me, and my knees buckled. As my vision fogged and tunneled, I could hear sirens in the distance, moving closer, far too late.

Stevens pulled the trigger.

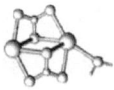

There were lights in the parsonage windows this time as I knocked on the door, wincing as the vibration snaked through my body and sent a lance of pain into my bandaged shoulder. Pastor Williams and his wife answered the door together.

Mrs. Williams was the antithesis of her husband, petite and delicate. "Thank you for coming, Mister Joseph," she said, as she helped me struggle out of my jacket. "It's been two weeks now, and she hasn't spoken a word. We thought maybe she'd talk to you, since you were...there...together."

Pastor Williams seemed shrunken, his face drawn, shoulders bent. "It's like the life's been sucked out of her," he murmured. "I've never seen her like this before. We've talked to her, prayed over her, tried to explain. She doesn't respond."

"I'll try," I said. "It was a terrible shock. No child should have to go through what she's experienced. I only wish I could have stopped him somehow."

The pastor gently laid his hand on my shoulder. "You did what you could, Darrin. No one can ask for more than that, and we're grateful."

"Thank you. That means a lot to me. Where is she?"

Mrs. Williams led me to a tiny bedroom where Penny lay under a white down comforter, flowers and stuffed animals crowding a table beside her bed. She didn't acknowledge my entrance; her eyes were open, fixed on some indistinct point on the ceiling.

I sat on the edge of the bed. "Hi, Penny. How're you doing?"

Silence.

I pressed on. "The doctor says I can go back to school next week, though I think it's going to be a while before I can play dodgeball again. Your friends are all asking about you."

She blinked, but maintained her focus on the ceiling as she said, on the verge of tears, her voice choked, "There was nothing there."

"Nothing where?"

"Inside the man. The man with the gun. I looked inside him for what would make him happy, and there was nothing there. It was cold, and dark, and empty."

"I think he lost hope, Penny. There wasn't any joy left in him."

"I killed him, Mister Joseph. I saw all that *nothing*, and then I realized that I was making it bigger, just being there with him, and I tried to make it stop, but I couldn't. I tried so hard, and then he...he..." Penny flung her arms around me and sobbed.

"It wasn't your fault," I whispered. "He came to the school knowing that was how it would end. There was no way to change his mind, no matter how hard you tried. He chose to take his own life. You didn't make it happen."

"But what good is it, if I can't even save one person, when it really matters? I thought I could fix *anybody*, Mister Joseph."

I gently turned her head so I could look her in the eye. "You did save somebody, Penny. You saved Joey and a whole room full of somebodies, including me. You stopped the man from thinking about us. You were very brave. Braver than anybody I know."

"I don't feel very brave."

"Brave people hardly ever know they're brave. But now, you've got to do the bravest thing of all."

"What's that?"

"Keep on living. Find your joy again and hold it close to you. Go back to making the world a little better for everyone you meet."

She sniffed and shook her head. "I don't think I can. After what happened, how can it ever be the same again?"

I'd been asking myself the same question for two weeks, and there was only one true answer. "It won't be the same, Penny, and it may never stop hurting, but that doesn't mean your life can't be as fine and good as before. I'll be around to help, and so will your parents, and your friends, and the people at your church, everyone whose life you've touched. Sometimes you don't save your world, Penny. Sometimes your world saves you."

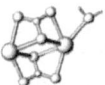

Fifteen years ago. Penny recovered, and we all recovered with her, though the scars, physical and otherwise, still itch from time to time, just so we don't forget them.

She was high school valedictorian, graduated from Auburn University summa cum laude in international affairs, and landed a job in Washington on our junior senator's staff, where she's earned a reputation as a problem-solver.

The children murmur and scribble, and the wasp departs the light fixtures to click stubbornly against a window, mere inches from escape.

I lean back in my chair and survey, for what must be the hundredth time, the framed picture Penny sent last week. It captures an historic moment: a table full of dignitaries, signing a peace treaty everybody said could never happen. She's standing in the background, among the diplomatic aides and other supporting players, a petite girl with a dazzling smile, playfully flashing a "V" for victory. There's a note handwritten on the photo's margin:

To my favorite teacher. Still saving the world, one smile at a time. Love, Penny.

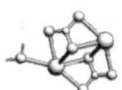

The girl blinked back a tear. It seems pain was not bound to any one world. She felt a longing in her chest, and she looked away.

"Tears are the mark of healing," said her master.

"No! I will not let it go. Not now…not ever. They killed my parents!" She clenched her fists and rerouted her sadness into the hate she loved. She rounded on her master. "I will avenge them, no matter how long it takes."

A flash of anger in Master Tok's eyes warned her she had crossed a line. But his face firmed and no rebuke came. "Learn." He pointed back to the pool.

She narrowed her eyes.

"LEARN!"

Begrudgingly, she turned back to the already icing pool of water. She saw another girl studying. A striking, black-haired girl about her own age.

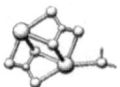

summer snaps

Keven Newsome

A deleted scene from the novel *Winter*

Winter raked her hand through her jet-black hair, forehead to crown. She gritted her teeth as she stared at the college Algebra homework on her desk. She traced the variables again with her pencil, willing the answer to emerge. But it didn't.

She slammed her pencil down and grunted. "I hate this!"

She got up and turned on the TV. Perhaps a few mind-numbing minutes of cartoons would help her concentrate. After grabbing a soda from the micro-fridge, she curled up in her papasan chair.

Something tingled at the base of her skull...a small nudging. She scratched the hairline at the back of her neck. Her eyes trained to her roommate's desk and to the jumble of keys and girly key chains sitting beside the pink laptop. Somehow she knew the keys were there, though Summer usually took them with her. *Why did she leave them? Whatever. None of my business.* She turned back to the TV and took a giant swig from her can.

A nudging...more urgent this time. Winter jumped out of the papasan as if prodded.

"Okay, stop it. I'm going. Geez. Leave me alone."

She took two giant steps toward Summer's desk and snatched up the keys. They clanked as they hit the bottom of the giant pocket on the thigh of her black cargo pants. She went back to her papasan, plopping down to more blissful procrastination.

A rattle of the doorknob made her turn. Summer walked in and tossed her backpack and flute case onto her frilly pink bed.

"Where have you been?" Winter asked.

"Practicing." Summer flicked her blonde hair over her shoulder and batted her perfectly painted eyes.

"Practicing what?"

"My flute of course. I have to practice everyday. That's part of being a music major." Summer tilted her head and raised her eyebrows as if Winter should have already known.

"Whatever," said Winter. "I need some help. Get over here."

Winter left comfort behind and went back to her desk. Summer grabbed her own desk chair and rolled it over.

"What's wrong?" Summer asked.

"This...I don't get how to solve for these stupid variables."

"When in doubt, cross multiply," Summer said.

"What?"

"It's something my teacher back home told us. Hold on." Summer grabbed Winter's text book and began flipping through the pages.

Winter leaned back and crossed her arms. "Why do we even need this class, anyway? I don't foresee me cross-multiplying for variables in everyday life."

"I don't know. They make everyone take it."

"It's stupid."

Summer laughed and tossed her hair. "Maybe. When is this due?"

"Friday," said Winter.

"Well, at least you have a couple of days."

Winter shook her head. "No, Summer. Tomorrow is Friday."

Summer stopped flipping pages and stared at her. Her face paled like a porcelain doll. "You mean today is Thursday?"

"Yeah. What did you think it was?"

"Oh no..." She jumped up and rushed to her backpack on the bed.

"What's wrong?"

"Today's my mom's birthday. I forgot to call her."

Winter laughed. "She'll forgive you."

Summer fished out her cell phone and stuck it to her ear. A moment later, her eyes widened and she pulled the phone away. She sank to her bed without having said a word.

"What's wrong?" Winter asked.

"Nobody's there," Summer whispered.

"They're probably just out."

"On a Thursday? No. Something's wrong."

Winter wasn't sure how to respond. She came to Summer's side and put an arm around her awkwardly. "I'm sure everything is fine, Summer."

"They never go out on Thursday. Something has to be wrong. I have to talk to them."

"Well, you said it was her birthday. Why wouldn't they go out?"

"They just…they just don't, okay?"

"I think you're overreacting just a little."

"You don't know them. I do. Don't tell me I'm overreacting!"

"Okay, sorry. Do they have a cell phone?"

Summer picked up her cell again and dialed. Her face changed from soap-white to sunburn-red. Tears ran down her cheeks. She pulled the phone back down after a few seconds.

"I'm going home," Summer said. She went to her desk and started looking around.

"Whoa! Wait a second. Let's just calm down a little."

Summer flung notebooks and papers to the ground. "Calm down? They might be hurt! Where are my keys?"

"You don't need them. Your parents are fine, Summer."

"WHERE ARE MY KEYS?" She attacked Winter's desk.

"Are you crazy? Stop this!" Winter stood, and Summer's keys clinked in her pocket.

Summer straightened and turned to stare at Winter. Her face glowed red and glistened with beads of sweat. Winter almost thought she saw steam rising from the sides of her head. Winter took a step back, a first when it came to her roommate. Summer advanced on her, and Winter backpedaled further.

"Where are my keys, Winter? You have them, don't you?"

"I…uh…"

"Give them to me!"

A warmth of knowing flooded Winter's mind. Suddenly, she could see exactly how the scene before her would unfold. A premonition. Hand.

Summer would put out her hand next.

Summer shoved out her hand.

I want them!

"I want them!" Summer shouted.

Hesitate. That's what the premonition said to do. So, Winter hesitated.

Summer stepped toward her, just as she was supposed to.

Winter let the premonition guide her through the next sequence of motions, playing out exactly what was supposed to happen. Lean. Shift weight. Look at the door. Look Summer in the eyes. Look at the far side of the room. Stare. Narrow eyes. Wait.

Out of the corner of her eyes, Winter saw Summer follow her gaze. Winter held her breath, waiting for Summer to take the two steps prescribed by the premonition. Summer turned and stalked two steps toward where Winter stared.

And when she did, Winter fled into the hall.

"Shanna!" Winter shouted. She could hear Summer pounding after her.

"Give me my keys! NOW!"

"SHANNA!"

"What's going on?" Shanna asked as she emerged from her Resident Assistant's room. Other girls poked their heads out of cracked doors.

"Summer's snapped! She's trying to go home!"

Summer jumped on Winter's back with an Amazon cry, and Winter fell to the hall floor.

"Give them to me!" Summer shrieked.

"No!"

Shanna grabbed Summer from behind. When she leaned back, both Summer and Winter came off the floor. A moment later, they crashed back down and Shanna fell on her backside.

"Calm down, Summer!" Shanna said, reaching to grab her again. "Let's talk about this first."

"I need to go home! Something's wrong, I need to go!"

Shanna leaned back, putting her full weight into pulling Summer, and Summer let go this time. Winter fell to the floor. Shanna and Summer flew backward and slammed to their backs.

"Now can we go talk?" Shanna asked, panting for air.

Winter rolled over and pushed herself up to sit against the wall.

Summer wept like a baby, almost to the point of hyperventilating.

Tears streaked her once-perfect makeup, making her look like a melting raccoon. "I need my mommy," she croaked.

"I know," Shanna said. She stood and pulled Summer to her feet.

"I tried calling, but she wouldn't answer." Summer leaned into Shanna's waiting arms, and sobbed.

"Come to my room. We'll try calling again." Shanna rolled her eyes at Winter as they passed.

Winter sprinted back to her room to retrieve her phone and call Kaci, their friend and small group leader at the Christian Life Center, for reinforcement. Doors closed in succession as the audience retreated back to their rooms, most of them laughing, but several looking homesick and already on cell phones. One girl lingered with crossed arms and a shower basket hanging from one hand.

"Freaks," the girl mumbled.

Winter gave her the most hateful glare she could muster. The girl returned one of her own, before prissing down the hall to the shower room.

An ember ignited in the bottom of Winter's stomach. Winter took a deep breath and let the fumes of the fire rise through her chest and into her mind. Past mistakes now presented themselves as possible options of retaliation. Winter knew this was an ungodly line of thought, but she didn't care. She enjoyed the feeling of power that anger and hate brought.

The base of her skull tingled again, and Winter gritted her teeth. "Fine." She shoved the contamination back into its cell.

Just before turning away and continuing to her room, Winter noticed that the girl had failed to pull her door completely to. She looked closer and saw the door was propped open purposefully by a shoe. Winter went over and kicked the shoe back into the room before her conscience could stop her. The door clicked shut, locking automatically. She smiled as the fire inside erupted with delight.

"What are you doing?"

Winter spun around to face Kaci. The fire froze over. "Uh, nothing. Just, um...I was about to call you."

"Shanna did. She said Summer went crazy and thought I might could help." Kaci brushed a strand of wavy brown hair out of her face.

"Yeah. I don't know what came over her." Winter shifted her eyes, avoiding Kaci's.

Kaci started walking down the hall. "Well, come on. Shanna can't handle that kind of drama by herself."

Winter followed. "I don't understand why Summer overreacted so much."

"She's not the only one who overreacts," Kaci said without turning.

Nudge. Winter hesitated. She turned and looked back at the locked door. Conflicting emotions battled between instinct and the right thing to do. She sighed, when the victor was not the one she wanted. Turning back, she sprinted to catch up.

"Um…can I borrow…"

"How did you stop Summer from leaving, anyway? I can't imagine that was easy." Kaci looked at her, brown eyes twinkling.

"I had her keys already…here in my pocket." Winter patted the bulge on her thigh and offered Kaci a sideways grin.

Kaci laughed. "How did you know?"

Winter shrugged. "Just a feeling, I guess."

Kaci held up her RA's master key.

Winter snatched it and looked at the floor. "Um…thanks. I'll be right back."

Kaci grinned. "I had a feeling."

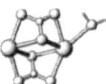

Guilt and anger collided. "I do not overreact!" Gizile shouted. "What is this place? What kind of magic is this? How does it know me?" She stood. "Why do we even linger? You teach me, but not what I need to know! I can use the ring now; I should be learning to wield it. Take me home."

When she turned, Master Tok was there with his arms crossed. He blocked her way with firmly planted feet. She saw the rebuke in her teacher's face.

"What is this?" she asked again, pointing to the pool.

He considered her a moment. "Aquasynthesis. A combining of worlds within a pool of water."

"And why did you bring me here?" There was more bite in the question than she intended, and she winced.

"For you to learn."

Realizing that he would not relent, she took a deep breath and forced the anger to dissipate. Guilt found its footing instead and she sank back to the rock. Gizile pulled her cloak tight again as a wave came in and ice exploded over the surface. Two young men approached a decrepit town...

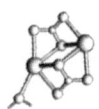

Faith's Fire

R. L. Copple

An excerpt from the novel *Reality's Dawn*

Seth turned his head my direction. "Hey Sisko, where are we going, exactly?"

I shrugged my shoulders. "I don't know."

He frowned. "After two years, you think I would know the answer. You're not one for making plans."

"God's making the plans, my friend. I'm just following along." I pointed to the city in the valley as we crested a hill. "But I can say we're going to that city over there. Know its name?"

Seth raised his hand to shield his eyes from the sun and grunted. "Yeah, it's an old backwater town called Dragon's Inn. Used to be a busy town named Crossroads, but fables of a dragon scared everyone away except for a few stalwart villagers. The name gradually changed when the dragon supposedly settled in these hills."

"I take it you don't believe this dragon exists?" I glanced to read his expression.

"Dragons? Really, I thought you wouldn't be taken in by old fables and superstitions." He chuckled.

"I've seen stranger things, like people turning into trees."

"Oh yeah, your steam-house story. Interesting tale, but more superstition if you ask me."

I shook my head and held up the ring on my finger. "Then how do you explain my ring, and the miracles God does through it?"

He stared at it. He couldn't deny the miracles he had watched me do, including those I had done on him and his sister, Gabrielle.

Gabrielle. Thoughts of her flooded my mind. How long before I could see her again? Would God ever finish with me so I could return to her?

Seth stared down the road again. "I guess God can use whatever He wants, but tell me why God would send a dragon to a village?"

I shrugged. "You'd have to ask Him, I guess. But God does use many things. You simply have to trust Him."

"Trust Him, huh? I've lived by my wits in the wild far longer than you've been away from mommy and daddy. The only one I've been able to trust is myself."

I chuckled. "All I can say is if you ever visit my village, do not use our steam house. You'll be very sorry."

"Sure, I'll keep that in mind." He pointed to the village gate a half-mile away. "But also keep in mind, this village is very superstitious. I wouldn't talk about your ring openly. Trouble would follow."

We entered the gate to see a few people milling around. They glanced up and scurried away as if not used to strangers. I saw older adults, but no children.

Occasionally, a creaking of rusty hinges would break the silence. Then the villager would jump back inside, slamming the door, knocking pieces of rotting wood onto their porch. Broken shutters swung in the wind and banged upon walls. Not a few houses had leaned slightly to one side. Maintenance hadn't been a high priority, apparently.

"There's the inn. I hope they have a good meal." Seth turned toward it.

I nodded, but the outside didn't seem too promising. The roof waved like a field of wheat in the wind, and holes dotted its surface. The dust swirled around us as we approached the door.

Inside, I squinted to see. At first, I thought the room seemed dark because my eyes needed to adjust. Yet a few seconds passed, and still I could only make out the outline of a counter. Little light penetrated here. A musty smell attacked my nostrils.

We crept to the counter and found a bell to ring. "Anyone here?" I heard something hit the floor, and then a small light flickered on. Soon, a bald-headed man wearing plain, brown clothing exited a room and shuffled to the counter.

"You be travelers, eh?" He squinted an eye at us.

"Yes, sir," I said. "We're hoping for a place to sleep and..." I scanned the room. "Maybe a meal?"

His mouth opened, and he had to grab the counter to keep from falling down. He bobbed up and down as if laughing, but only a slight wheeze pierced the dank air. After he collected himself, he said, "I have a room you can bed down in, but your meal won't come from here."

Seth frowned at me. "Forget why God sent a dragon here, why did He send *us* here?"

The old man coughed, and the laughter fizzled to a loud whisper. "Oh, you know about the dragon, do you?" He pointed a long, thin finger at us. "If I were you, I would get right on out of town. The dragon don't take too kindly to strangers."

Seth grunted. "I told you they were superstitious. I would rather sleep outside than in here anyway. Let's go."

He grabbed at my hand, but I pulled back. "Sir, when's the last time you saw this dragon?"

"Well..." He scratched his head and stared at the counter. "Been a long time. A very long time. Can't say I recall seeing the dragon. But he's out there. Don't you make no bones about that."

The door to the inn slammed open, flooding the room with light. A young woman stood backlit in the doorway. "Doctor, hurry." She paused as if noticing us for the first time, but continued. "It's the baby. She's coughing up blood."

"I'll be right there," the old man said, and he shuffled back to his room.

I blurted out, "You're the doctor too?"

"You betcha, boy. There's not a lot of people here, you know. We do what we're able."

It dawned on me why I had seen no children. Few lived long enough. Sadness filled my heart for these people, trapped in time and superstitions, condemning them to a life of rot and decay. I knew I should go with him.

Seth pulled on me again. "Come on, let's get out of here."

I held up my hand. "Not yet. We need to go see this baby."

The old man shuffled from behind the counter and headed to the door. "No need, boy. It's the sickness. They all die from it."

"What sickness?" He sounded so ho-hum about it.

He stopped and turned. His eyes blinked as if they had cried for years, and the tear-well had run dry. "Dragon sickness."

"Dragon sickness?" Seth's eyes widened. "I told you they were superstitious."

"We're still coming with you, sir." I opened the door for him.

"Guess I can't stop you. It's your life you'll be risking. Have it your way." He hobbled out the door.

We arrived at the house and entered. While still darker than I would have liked, at least rays of sunlight shot through the windows and blanketed the floor in patterns. The doctor leaned over the crib and examined the baby.

The woman, red-haired and around thirty years old, stared at the baby, occasionally glancing at the doctor. "Can she survive?"

He shook his head. "Afraid not, Cherie. Too far gone, this one. There's nothing I can do for her." He put a hand on Cherie's shoulder.

She hung her head and closed her eyes. Her shoulders slumped. A vision of Gabrielle crying over our own baby pierced me, and I stopped breathing for a second.

I knew then why God had brought me here: to banish this dreadful disease from these people. And it would start with this baby. "I can help."

Seth grabbed my arm. The others turned their heads, disbelief written in their eyes. Yet, they parted. They had done all they could; why not let the fool have a shot?

I pushed Seth's hand from my arm. "It's all right, I'm meant to do this." I moved to the cradle. The low light revealed a pale figure. Bones thrust themselves against sagging skin, and a trail of dried blood ran from a corner of the girl's mouth. I placed my hand upon the child. "Father, banish the sickness from this baby and town."

For a moment, the baby remained still, and seconds ticked by. Then, a breath sucked in, and a cry rang from the lungs. Color returned to the body, and her eyes opened.

I lifted the infant from the crib and handed her to Cherie. "I believe the child is hungry."

Her eyes beamed as she received the child. She hugged the baby to her chest and cried tears of joy, the first in many years, no doubt. Warmth filled my being at her reaction.

I turned to see the reaction of the other villagers who had watched. An audience had gathered outside the door. They murmured as the news of what had happened spread. But their reaction surprised me.

"Sorcery, that's what this is. Black magic." The doctor pointed his crooked finger at me. "You'll bring down the wrath of the dragon upon us, boy." Fear etched lines upon his sagging face. Those in the room backed away.

"No, God did this, not me." Couldn't they understand? Why would they not trust in what God had done?

"God has refused to answer our prayers for years, boy. Why would your prayer be any different? It's magic, I tell you." He motioned for some men to bind me. "We must sacrifice you before the dragon takes our whole village."

Affirmations arose among the people, and they pressed in to grab me. Seth pressed toward me, shoving people to the ground.

I held up my hand. "No Seth, these people should not be hurt."

He paused for a moment. Doubt filled his eyes. "But—" A pot cracked over his head, and he slumped to the floor. A small swarm of villagers pushed me from the house while others pulled Seth's body into the street.

People jeered and spit upon me. Some hit me, and welts formed on my body. Could I have heard God wrong? Should I have listened to Seth? Questions flowed through my mind as the crowd shoved me to a series of wooden beams sprouting from the ground, topped with crossbeams. The aged rope and weathered wood indicated they hadn't done this in many years.

They placed us under two of the beams and tied our wrists with ropes anchored to the top. They fastened my feet firmly against the beams where they entered the ground.

The crowd moved away and left us there, spread-eagle, awaiting…I didn't know what. They kept crying out "sorcery" and "wizard" in accusation, as if arguing with a judge in their heads about their innocence.

Yet they did not attempt to kill us. They waited.

In the midst of the jeering, Seth awoke. "Oh, my head." He pulled on the ropes. "What's going on?"

"I think we're being sacrificed, as best I can tell."

"Sacrificed!" He yanked harder against the ropes; his bulging muscles tightened with the effort. Yet, the cords did not give to his strength. He ended his struggle with a cry of resignation and slumped on the ropes. "I don't want to be a sacrifice!"

"Calm down. I'm sure God has a plan. He got us into this, He'll get us out." I hoped. Somewhere within me, I felt this would not end in death.

"What is this plan of His? Why is He doing this?" Seth's voice echoed against the buildings in the street, and the crowd quieted for a moment in response.

I turned my head and locked onto Seth's eyes. Fear born of helplessness raged in them. "I don't know, but He does. However this turns out, His will be done."

He looked at me as if I had lost my mind, but at the same time, I could sense in his soul a desire for such confidence. He stared at me for a long minute until the sound of footsteps interrupted our wordless conversation.

Not human footsteps, but those of a large animal. We both searched in the direction the sound originated, yet nothing could be seen. I heard hard breathing while the ground shook louder and louder with each pounding step as it approached. Still, the beast remained cloaked to my eyes.

In contrast to my talk, the sound and feeling of death approaching tensed my body to flee despite the fact my bonds wouldn't allow it. My legs shook and could barely hold me up.

I felt a caustic breath flowing over me. The creature must be right in front of me, yet it remained invisible. The man told the truth when he said he had never seen it.

The noise of the crowd had disappeared as they waited for the final blow. The creature turned to Seth who cried prayers of mercy. Then the breath returned before me, and the creature materialized before my eyes.

I wished it had remained invisible.

Cries and screams erupted from the crowd, and many ran for safety. My insides turned to water.

A brownish-red head, much like a huge lizard, hung inches from my face. A long neck held up the head. Its flattened body supported wings of skin spanning several feet. It gently flapped them in the wind as if cooling itself. It lifted its head and roared. My body vibrated.

During the roar, I heard shouts of "No!" and "Get away!" from the crowd cowering behind fences and walls. I felt the ropes give way. Seth had already been cut down, and he rushed off toward the crowd. I turned to see Cherie, shaking, holding a sword. She thrust it into my hand. "God be with you." Then she darted away. Genuine love makes heroes from the most unexpected of people.

I turned back as the dragon lowered its head. I had to keep the dragon's attention on me and not on those escaping.

"Sisko, run!" I heard Seth's voice yell from the crowd.

Right. I would be roasted before I could move five steps.

The dragon stared me in the eyes. It lifted its head once again, but this time it inhaled deeply. Everything in me said, "Flee now, this is your only chance." But another calm and sure voice said, "Stay. Your work is not done."

So I stayed. Maybe my death would teach the villagers a lesson. Maybe they would feel sorry and never sacrifice anyone else. The head came down, the mouth opened wide, and I saw the flames forming in its throat and erupting from its open jaws.

I closed my eyes and threw my arm over my head. I heard a loud roar and the sound of crackling wood all around me. Yet I felt no heat, only a cool breeze. Dew formed on my forehead. I put my arm down and opened my eyes. A blanket of flames flowed around me as if it caressed my body and enlivened my soul. After a few seconds, the flames ended.

The dragon reared its head back in confusion. The wooden beams around me crackled with flames. The tip of my sword glowed red from the heat. Yet, my clothing remained untouched, and my hair felt wet as if I had just washed it.

The dragon reared its head back again and blasted another round of fire at me. Again, I felt a cool and dewy breeze while everything else around me burned.

The dragon brought its head back toward me and sniffed. I reached out and caressed its snout. Oddly enough, I heard something akin to a purr. I smiled, and I could have sworn it smiled back.

An impression entered my mind, an impression that I should ride this dragon. I leapt upon its back, and we launched into the air.

Like a soaring bird, we raced into the clouds as the wind whipped though my hair. Perched on the back of such a beast, clinging to its neck, I experienced something few men have: a new perspective on life, both freeing and threatening.

During the ride, the dragon's thoughts and feelings erupted into my mind. I felt its sadness and its rage, but mostly its bewilderment at the villagers. It had been brought to them as a curse, but they had failed to learn from it.

The ride seemed long and yet ended before I wanted it to. The dragon landed back on the village street. I dismounted and petted its back. Then it shot into the sky with a deafening roar. It disappeared over the hills, returning to some forgotten land. It had finished its task.

Seth rushed toward me and nearly knocked me over with his hug. "Sisko, I thought the dragon had fried you for its supper, but like you said, God did have a plan." His eyes blazed from within, as if some spark had ignited a fire.

I had to laugh. "Yes, beyond my wildest thoughts."

I turned to face the crowd as they exited their hiding places. The doctor approached and squinted one eye at me. "Who are you?"

A pointless question. I pointed at the church spiral in the center of the village. "Where's your priest?"

He bowed his head. "He did a miracle, and then the dragon came. We believed he caused it and forced him to leave."

I shook my head. "The dragon said he came because of your reaction to the miracle, and you failed to repent."

Cries erupted from the crowd. "How could we have been so blind?" "We were wrong." "God have mercy on us!"

"You're no different than many whose faith is misplaced." I focused on the doctor. His long face expressed his struggle. "Isn't that right, Doctor?"

He glanced at me, and I saw pride break in his eyes as tears formed. He fell to the ground, joining in the sorrow for past sins.

Yet, it didn't take long for the crowd's sorrow to swell into joyfulness. The crowd clamored to thank me. Next thing I knew, I had been lifted onto their shoulders and carried away.

They celebrated that evening. The Church shone with light, and though no priest officiated, the people rejoiced and worshiped as best they could. Cherie, with her baby, stood at the front, a smile on both their faces. The angels surely rejoiced with us. A smoldering ember had finally ignited into a full fire of life, and a living village emerged from the ruins.

Seth and I hiked up the mountain trail. We breathed hard in the thin air. After reaching the top, we rested on the peak. The valley of Dragon's Inn lay on one side, in a sea of green. On the other, a barren land of rock and shrub spread for many miles. We each took a swig of our water.

"So where are we headed now?" Seth grinned.

I wished I could say back to his house and Gabrielle. I scanned the wilderness and swung my finger toward a group of distant hills, barely visible across the plains. "Out there, somewhere."

Seth grinned. I had the distinct feeling he would follow me to the end of the world. And he might very well be required to, but in a way he didn't expect.

"Let's get moving then. We don't want to be up here when nightfall hits." I grabbed my pack and hoisted it on my shoulders.

Where would God take us now? I couldn't wait to find out.

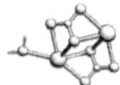

Gizile sighed. Her guilt had melted into a melancholy as cold and gray as the weather. God. She wanted to trust Him...to trust anyone. Why was it so hard to let go? Why was it so hard to believe? She looked up at her master, self-consciously rubbing the dragon runes on her arms. He was the only person who had never let her down. She sighed again and stared out to sea, a piece of her hoping to see dark, wide wings beat the air...a dragon of her own, come to consume her for her unbelief. The water below crackled. She looked down in time to see the next vision begin.

What was this? A structure of some-sort flying through the heavens? Gizile forgot her melancholy and leaned closer. Surely it was not made of stone. Perhaps bronze or steel?

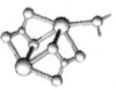

the unjust judge

Adam Graham

Space Marshal Dan Morris looked up as his gray office door swished up on Space Station Zeta VI. Father Michael strode in, decked in a white clerical collar with an otherwise black suit. He dragged along a weeping gray-skinned female humanoid dressed in the traditional golden robe of the species at the top of the food chain on the planet Vagonia.

Dan picked up his datapad and sighed at the holographic moon yacht it displayed. If only he could buy it now. Unfortunately, that would arouse the suspicion of the United Planets that he'd been taking kickbacks for undercharging customs. They were kind of particular about that. He'd have to wait a few years to spend the money.

Father Michael tapped his foot on the carpeted floor. "Marshal!"

Dan grunted. "What is it?"

Father Michael crossed his arms. "This woman's husband has been shot down in cold blood, and her husband's cargo ship has been stolen."

Dan put his hands together in a pyramid. "Too bad for her."

The gray-skinned alien freak blinked twice and lowered her jaw so her unduly long frog tongue dropped out past her chin.

Father Michael raised an eyebrow. "What are you going to do about it?"

Dan kicked back in his chair and put his hands behind his head. "Nothing."

130

"But you're the law."

Dan chuckled. "If I choose to enforce it."

Father Michael huffed. "I'll report you to United Planets Command."

"You do that. It took them nine months to find someone to take on your little hellhole." Though it was ironic to be one of the good guys for a change—at least compared to most of the scum that lurked around here. "As long as the Merlocks don't invade and I keep space around here reasonably clear of pirates, they don't care about time-consuming investigations."

"But we know who did it. It was Ben Chou."

Dan smirked. "Thank you. Now I'm definitely not going to do anything. Chou is a human being, and I doubt that her husband was."

"He was Vagonian."

Dan clucked his tongue. "Explains everything. Vagonians are asking to be shot."

The gray alien with the freakishly long tongue trembled and wept.

Father Michael jumped back like his feet had been shot at. "Marshal, that's bigotry."

Dan waved this off. "Nonsense. I believe in human rights. Not rights for every bipedal alien smart enough to fly a spaceship, but whose government can't be bothered to pay their dues in the United Planets. Why don't you keep your superstition to Earth?"

"The Pope had determined that the Vagonians and dozens of other lifeforms carry the image of God just like humans. Tella and Pul Chezero were some of my first converts."

"So, the Pope says it?" Dan smirked. "Up here, the Pope is an old man in a ridiculous hat."

The alien pointed her finger. "You are God's minister for justice and you don't do justice."

"Please. I don't care about God."

"I love my husband very much."

"Good for you."

The alien blew out a gust of wind. "You must avenge me."

Dan yawned. "Avenge yourself. I'd be happy to loan you a blaster, but Chou's an Earth Citizen, so that wouldn't look good. But surely you could find some way, a poison chalice, or your ceremonial killing knives."

"No, vengeance is not mine, but the Bible says you bear the sword.

You must do justice."

Dan leaned forward. He had more boats to look at. "Alien, forget it."

"No, you are God's minister. You must do justice."

"You're a broken music implant, alien."

The alien stomped and shook a fist. "You must do justice."

"Padre, get her out of here."

Father Michael folded his arms. "She's not a child. She can handle herself."

He flounced out. Coward.

The alien whimpered and clasped her hands. "Please, my husband never hurt anyone."

"I don't care."

"Chou stole our ship and without it, I'm destitute and stranded here."

"Again, I don't care."

"Avenge me."

"No, now get out of my office."

"I'll be back."

Dan grunted and returned to his moon yachts.

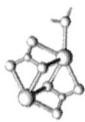

Dan manipulated the data on his wallscreen using his Igloves' holographic keyboard.

The alien slipped in. "Do justice, for you are the minister of God."

Dan pointed a gloved finger at the door. "Get out and stay out."

"This is a public place. Father Michael said I have the right to be here."

"He's correct. You could appeal to a United Planet Court. Unfortunately, the nearest United Planet Court is eight star systems away, so I'm the judge, and I consider this an obstruction of the operation of the marshal's office."

She glowered. "Avenge me."

Dan jumped up, grabbed her arm, and pulled the alien across the floor to the detention cell. He pressed a button to deactivate the forcefield and tossed her inside. "Cool off."

He turned the forcefield back on.

She slammed her fists against the forcefield. "Avenge me! Avenge me!"

"Computer, soundproof jail."

The woman's frog tongue protruded from her mouth with the silent screams.

Dan smiled. "Good old twenty-third century technology."

The gray woman formed letters with her arms like she was a cheerleader at a Space Polo match. A-V-E-N-G-

Dan glanced away, glowering. He stomped back to his desk.

A few minutes later, he glanced over at the forcefield. She was pacing now, her lips pressed together into a thin line.

She fell and flopped all over the ground. A seizure. He gulped. He didn't even know what to do with one of these things. If he got a dead prisoner in here, the paperwork was going to kill him.

He needed a doctor. "Computer, transport Father Michael Pilchard, emergency code eight-seven-bee-three-four."

Father Michael, the only on-board doctor, raced in wielding a tennis racket, and wearing a pair of white gym shorts. He squinted and blinked. "Marshal, I really would rather you not do that."

"It's an emergency. Your little annoyance got herself thrown in a detention cell, and now she's having some type of seizure."

Father Michael sped to the cell. Dan lowered the shield. The woman writhed on the floor towards them. She jumped up and pointed a finger at Dan. "Do justice."

Dan scowled. "You faked this? All right, that's it. You get out of detention, but I'm going to set the bio-detection scanners at my office door, which will kill you if you step inside here."

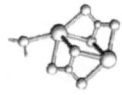

The salty perfume of french fries and greasy burgers permeated Rosie's Earth Cafe, a small on-station joint set in the robotic silver architecture of the mid-twenty-second century. Dan settled into an uncomfortable iron booth and hunched over the plastic menu. Personally, he preferred the padded seats back in style on Earth, but real food was worth a little discomfort. Better than choking down another computer-generated facsimile of a burger from his office food generator or any of the dozen weird places that catered to the aliens' tastes.

Footsteps came closer and stopped behind him.

Dan flipped through the menu. "I'll take baby back ribs and an order of McDonald's fries."

"Avenge me!"

Dan whirled and glared at the crazy widow. "You get out of here or I'll have you thrown out."

The alien wagged her tongue at him and stormed out. A waiter rushed over. "So sorry, sir."

"Baby back ribs and McDonald's fries." Dan grunted and looked out the window, to a promenade deck decorated to resemble a brick city street dotted with maple trees.

The alien marched into the middle of the street and held up a sign with "Do Justice, Marshal" written in six languages. Half a dozen people stopped to gawk at her.

Great, she'd draw everyone on the station here.

The waiter brought the steaming food. Thick barbeque sauce soaked the baby back ribs, real butter drenched the broccoli, and enough salt saturated the French Fries to preserve them through a nuclear winter. It was enough to make his mouth water—usually.

Dan stared at the plate, at the sign outside, and the growing crowd. Couldn't a man even eat in peace? "Waiter, give me a container to take this home."

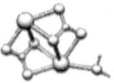

A continuous beeping at his door awoke Dan in his quarters at 0300 hours. He shuffled across the white carpeting, past the salamander-shaped pink couch, to the door, and hit the button. The door slid up into the wall.

The persistent devil of an alien widow stood outside. "Avenge me."

"Go get to sleep."

"I can't sleep while justice isn't done for my husband. Neither shall you."

Dan screamed and punched the button to shut the door.

The beeping continued incessantly, all night long.

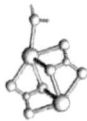

Dan strode through the gray halls of the Space Station loading docks. A nine-foot-tall green Merrickian approached towards him hauling a quarter ton of wheat. Dan stood aside. The Merrickian leered and sauntered on past.

Father Michael ran up. "There you are, Marshal. I've been looking all over for you."

Dan grunted. "Sorry you found me."

"First of all, I researched it, and a bio-detection scanner is a device that scans for lifeforms in general. It's not used for office security."

Dan chuckled. "Give the boy in the black suit a gold star. Let him who hasn't made up technobabble to sucker a layman cast the first space rock."

"I'll have you know I've got a report ready to send out detailing your failure to investigate the death of Pul Chezero."

Dan sighed. "I'm going to get Chou right now."

"Because of my complaint?"

Dan shook his head. "The day I take action based on the fear of a bad report from a part-time medical adjunct is the day I turn in my space blaster."

"So God did get through to you?"

Dan laughed. "Oh, give me a break! I'm not afraid of your precious bronze age deity. That alien is exhausting me with her constant demands. I've got to give her justice before she drives me crazy."

They walked down the corridor and took a right at a dock that had Ben Chou's name on it in green letters. Chou climbed the steps into his ship.

Dan waved. "Chou! Your flight's been grounded. Get over here."

Chou climbed out of his spaceship and trotted across the departure bay. "Marshal, I'm not carrying contraband. At least none that I'm not willing to pay the appropriate fees for."

Shucks. He could have put that money towards his moon yacht. Dan cleared his throat. "Chou, you're under arrest on suspicion of murder and grand theft."

"I've not killed anyone. Only a few aliens."

"Intergalactic law doesn't make a distinction between humans and aliens. You don't get open season on any species. And if they're capable of speaking a discernible language, it's murder."

"Maybe, but I have a few more hunts left in me. "Chou raised his hand and on it was an illegal palm blaster.

Was that what Chou shot the widow's husband with? Dan reached for his blaster.

Chou fired. Dan flew backwards, banged into a hard metal surface, and the world vaporized.

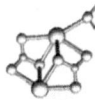

Dan took a breath as he lay stretched out on a firm mattress with all the softness of carpeting. His head and chest felt like a Merrickian had stomped on him. He opened his eyes. A medicine cabinet lay three or four meters away. To his right, a machine monitored his vital signs. Oh great, the infirmary. Hopefully, he wouldn't have to eat here. Infirmary food made retail computer-generated food edible.

Father Michael leaned down over him. "Marshal, welcome back. We weren't sure you were going to be rejoining us for a while."

"What happened to Chou?"

Father Michael opened his suit jacket and showed him a holstered taser. "Self-defense. A deputy remanded him to a detention cell and recovered Tella's spaceship."

Dan groaned. Saved by the priest? Better to have died than have to live this down. "How long have I been out?"

"Three days. You're alive, though with that blast, the odds were against you. But I have my own theory as to why you recovered."

"Oh let me guess. Your prayers."

"No, not mine, Tella's. When she found out you'd been critically wounded trying to bring her justice, she prayed for you. You wouldn't believe it. I've never seen anyone pray so constantly. She was here for sixty hours straight."

"Padre, I believe it."

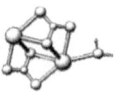

Adapted from Luke 18:1-8

And the Lord said, "Hear what the unjust judge saith.

And shall not God avenge His own elect, who cry day and night unto Him, though He bear long with them?

I tell you that He will avenge them speedily. Nevertheless when the Son of Man cometh, shall He find faith on the earth?" —Luke 18:6-8 (KJV)

"No! He can't!" she shouted.

Master Tok grunted in confusion.

"I can't let God do it. I have to avenge them!"

"Was vengeance the lesson you saw? Not seeking God?"

"Easy for you to spout advice! To show a vision that quotes from a Holy Book! You don't understand…this is my burden…they were my *parents*."

"And they were my friends."

Gizile looked at him. He stared off to sea, his face drooping. The flame inside her fizzled. "I…I'm sorry," she said. "But do you think that God…"

His expression didn't change, but there *was* a twinkle. Two minds with but a single thought. He gestured downward again.

"GET OUT," came a voice from the pool. Gizile jerked back around. The vision had already begun.

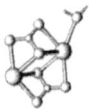

dry places

Travis Perry

"GET OUT," the voice boomed.

Out the door tumbled Gusano, indignant.

It wasn't really a door; it *was* an entryway, but it didn't have hinges or a doorknob or any of the usual "door" things. Nor did Gusano really pick himself up from the sand and dust himself off.

It wasn't really sand and he didn't really dust himself, but it was something like that. It was a dry place, much like a sand-strewn desert, and Gusano separated his being from the dryness, swipe by swipe, in preparation for escaping the area.

Gusano swore a stream of profanity. He trotted away from the alien entity behind him, the one who'd been his home for several years now.

He hated this dimension. Well, it wasn't really another dimension in the sense of length, width, height. It was more like "Another Dimension" as done so often in Science Fiction.

There was no sun, yet the sky blazed hot, no real sand, yet so gritty. Gusano thirsted for anything to quench the dryness in his throat, yet there was nothing to drink.

"Too bad you can't die of thirst here!" he muttered. His trot had become a trudge.

He could see other aliens partly submerged into the landscape, immense, nearly translucent beings, whose slow thoughts sparked like bright lights in their cavernous heads. Gusano knew if you could catch one of these sparks, you'd know what the creature was thinking. As if he cared.

The only thing Gusano cared about was getting out of this dryness and the only way to do that was to find a door into one of the aliens. He didn't care about exploring, though the appeal of adventure was partly how he'd gotten himself into this mess. They'd promised adventure, "a Great and Noble Struggle," along with glory. Gusano would get his proper due.

He kicked the dryness, "sand" flying. He'd like to kill the seven jerks who'd talked him into this. Seven guys he'd thought were intelligent and competent. So he'd gone along with the Plan. Then they'd abandoned him.

He imagined himself killing them slowly, one by one. He couldn't decide which he'd kill first. Or if he'd like to do them in simultaneously. He treasured these thoughts. A knife in the gut to this one. Strangulation for that one. Boiling for the biggest. He replayed it over and over as he walked, changing the details, trying to find a formula that would satisfy him. Not that he would actually be able to do what he dreamed of, anyway.

Gusano realized that his kicking and imaginary fighting had him stumbling like a madman.

"So what," he answered himself. "There's no one here who can see me."

He stopped in front of one of the alien beings. He groped around for the door and found it, but it was locked. And he didn't have the key. Gusano swore again.

The being never noticed his presence; it just elephantinely continued doing whatever it was doing.

These were aliens in one way, but if you could slow yourself down to their speed and see things through their eyes, they experienced the world much the same as Gusano. So in a way, they were *not* aliens.

He stumbled away from that one, and on to the next nearest alien. He couldn't get in there either. He tried another, still no luck. Off in the distance, he saw a fourth. Maybe, just maybe, it would be unlocked.

With each step, heaviness weighed him down so he felt like he sank in the "sand" like the aliens. He gave up and plopped down to rest. But the "sand" scorched too hot to be comfortable. He rolled over several times, trying to find a cooler spot, but there was none. He staggered to his weary feet again. Loneliness made him wish anyone could be there with him— even if it were one of the seven.

A thought of his old home drifted into his mind with a pang for the lost luxury. *Maybe I should go back where I came from. Maybe the voice that drove me out is gone now.*

And he still had the key.

He trudged through more blazing "other dimension," a glimmer of hope in his heart. Maybe he'd find some rest after all, some coolness. When he got back to it after an indeterminate amount of time, he saw the being had moved, but not far. For a brief moment, he was filled with fear that the lock had changed. But it hadn't—he was in.

There were membranes that marked different areas inside the alien, different rooms if you will. When he'd lived there before, he'd kicked these around quite a bit. And he'd captured thoughts and thrown them around, just for fun. And tracked in dryness, too.

Now the place was neat and clean, back the way it was when he first moved in. It was a big place too; he'd forgotten how big.

It was comfortable, but its uncluttered size reminded him of how lonely he was. This loneliness drove him outside, where he whispered a message into the dry wind.

The knock came, he couldn't have said how much later. He nervously opened the door.

The seven stood out there.

"Hey, fellas!" said Gusano. "I thought I'd invite you over to my place, all fixed up and cleaned out—just to, just to let bygones be bygones, you know? I think you'll like it."

"Oh, don't worry yourself about that," answered the biggest, "I think we'll LOVE your place. It even comes with its own little live-in slave!" A wicked grin spread across his face.

Gusano swallowed, hard.

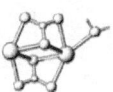

"When the unclean spirit is gone out of a man, he walks through dry places, seeking rest; and finding none, he says, I will return unto my house whence I came out. And when he comes, he finds it swept and garnished. Then goes he, and takes to him seven other spirits more wicked than himself; and they enter in, and dwell there: and the last state of that man is worse than the first."
—Luke 11:24-26 (author's translation)

Confusion overwhelmed her. "What was I to learn from that? That evil longs for vengeance?"

Master Tok considered her question, his finger tracing a circle in the cold sand. His eyes met hers. "How does evil consider itself, child? As evil?"

Her conscience aroused itself and Gizile found herself performing a quick inventory of her own trespasses. She silently recited a short prayer and calmed.

"I am sorry, Master Tok...for my behavior."

He merely grunted.

"Perhaps," she said, "it would be better for all if I did grow old enough to learn to use the ring. I will do better. My emotions will not overtake me again."

She heard a mutter, and turned. But her master was still-faced and staring at the clouds.

The sound of water rushing into the pool made her turn back. When the ice had formed, she saw a man at a table. A man weeping. She felt a tug at her heart and at the corners of her eyes.

Another muttering from her master. She tuned her surroundings out, and allowed herself to be absorbed into another vision.

the assistant

Keven Newsome

William supported his head with the palms of his hands, elbows resting on the table. Tears ran unhindered down his forearms as his body convulsed. An unopened beer sat on the table to his left...a .45 to his right.

Nothing else mattered. Either choice would suffice.

A figure stepped out of the shadows, a handsome man with slick black hair. He wore a black trench coat and dark sunglasses. Smiling with one side of his mouth, he stepped to William's side. With one finger he touched the small puddle of tears collecting on the table. His smile deepened.

"It doesn't have to be this way," the man said as he moved behind William. He put his hands on William's shoulders and squeezed. "You can end this anytime you like."

He moved his hands to William's cheeks and lifted, guiding him to look beyond the tears. "Have you forgotten the gun? Why must you continue to be so miserable? Pick it up. End this now."

William sniffed and the tears stopped. He stared at the gun. His fingers twitched toward it.

The man moved to the other side of the table and knelt behind the gun in William's line of sight. "It won't even hurt. Just a gentle squeeze of the trigger, and all this pain goes away."

William tore his eyes from the gun and put his head back in his hands.

"What are you waiting for? They're not coming back. You're alone."

William reached for the beer and pulled the tab. He threw his head back and guzzled for several seconds.

The man stood up and circled the table. "Go ahead. Numb the pain, but it'll be back. You know I'm right. And what are you going to do then? You can't stay drunk your entire life. Think about it."

William set the can down and stared at the table.

"Let the alcohol work through your system. It'll make this easier."

The man knelt by William's side and leaned close to his ear. "Don't you want to be with them again? Don't you want to see your son? Your daughter?" He leaned in and whispered. His lips almost brushed William's ear. "Your wife?"

He stood and started circling again. "You miss them. You miss their voices, their presence. They left you. They left you... alone." The last word seemed to echo from the walls of the kitchen.

William's fingers flexed toward the gun, though he continued to stare elsewhere.

The man smiled, curling his lip. "You could be with them in only a few moments. It would be quick. Why wait? They would want you to. They want to see you again. They're waiting."

William's hand moved a little.

The man stepped closer and loomed over William. "You can be happy again. You can end the pain."

William moved his hand further.

"Do it! Now!"

William grabbed the gun and pulled it close, holding it to his chest with both hands.

The man knelt again. "Don't worry. I'm here to help. I'll talk you through it. I've done this many times. I was there to help your wife." He put a hand on William's arm. "The important thing is for you not to listen to the lies. No matter what anyone else has said, no matter what your instincts tell you, you need to realize that it was your fault, just as you suspect.

"If you had been a better father, your daughter wouldn't have run away and gotten into trouble. If you had loved her more, she wouldn't have sought love elsewhere. If you had been a better father, your son wouldn't have had to go help. Instead, you went back to your beer. You failed your daughter by not being there. You failed your son by not doing the job yourself. At least I was there when they died. Where were you? They died slowly and painfully as the car burned to the ground, screaming for help that wouldn't arrive. Does that help?"

William caressed the gun like a newborn baby.

"And your wife couldn't take it, could she? She was an emotional wreck. She needed you to be strong. She needed you to comfort her. But did you? No. You comforted the alcohol instead." The man put his hand over William's hand on the gun. "At least she left you plenty of bullets, my friend."

William looked up to the faint red stain on the wall next to him, streaked from scrubbing with bleach.

"You see?" said the man in black. "It was your fault. Go to them now... apologize. It's the right thing to do. It's only fair."

William started shaking.

"Yes... it's time. Do it."

William lifted the gun, his whole arm lurching.

"DO IT!"

William dropped the gun on the table.

The man in black stood and leaned into William's face and shouted. "What's wrong with you? Do you enjoy misery? Do you enjoy blood on your hands? You're worthless! You're a fool! You're a waste of a human being! End this... put the world out of the misery of your existence, before you kill someone else. It's the only honorable thing to do. Blow your brains out. End the pain. DO IT!"

William started to convulse. He grabbed the end of the table and shook it, screaming as loud as he could. The contents of the table slid away and crashed to the floor... including the gun.

"Idiot. Pick it up! What's wrong with you? You're a disgrace. You can't even kill yourself with dignity. You're a failure at everything. Pick it up! NOW!"

William fell to the ground weeping. He crawled beneath the table for a moment. When he stood he held two items, the gun and a package. As he sat, he placed them both before him.

"What's that?" asked the man.

William pulled off an envelope taped to the package and opened it. He pulled out a card that read "Happy Father's Day" on the front.

The man in black huffed. "Father's Day was last month. This is a waste of your time. Finish this…finish it before you lose the nerve."

William opened the card and a letter fell out.

"Don't read that," said the man. "It's from a dead person. It will do you no good. Just pick up the gun and let's end this. I'm here with you. We're doing this together, remember? Forget the letter."

William grabbed the letter and opened it. The man crossed his arms and paced. As William read, somehow he found more tears. At the end, he slammed the letter down, took up the package, and tore through the wrapping.

After holding the book in his hands for a moment, he placed it on the table next to the gun.

"A Bible? Are you kidding me?" said the man in black as he returned to the table. "That's the coward's way out! If God cared about you, why would you have lost your family? If he really existed, why do you hurt right now? Your son was a fool to leave this for you. It changes nothing! A Bible can't bring your family back. A Bible can't heal the pain!"

He knelt and put a hand on William's shoulder. "But the gun can… pick it up. No more wasting time with all this crying. Nothing else can save you. Splatter your brains on the wall with your wife's, and you can join her in Hell. That's where you belong… that's what you deserve. It's too late for you, it's too late to change your life. End it now! Pick it up!"

He leaned into William's face.

"The gun… GET IT! Now! Stop thinking about it, you worthless piece of trash! Stop the pain, stop your existence! Do it! DO IT!"

William convulsed again. His body rocked with sobs and his hand reached for the gun.

The man threw his arms in the air and laughed. "YES! Do it! Put it to your head! Blow away the pain! Blow away your sorrows!"

William's shaking arm bent and the barrel moved to his temple.

"That's it… yes," the man hissed in ecstasy. "Death, sweet death. Do it! DO IT!"

Suddenly, William held his breath and stopped trembling. The gun settled into place on the side of his head.

The man in black started to dance around the table, laughing.

William took a deep steadying breath… then slammed the gun back to the table. His hands went for the Bible.

"NOOOO!" the man screamed, rushing to William's side. "What are you doing? Put that down!"

William opened it to the bookmark left there by his son.

"Stop this! This won't help, put it down! NOW! The gun... get the gun!"

He started reading.

The man in black put his hands to his head and roared. "NO! Don't do this! You can't... you can't... you're mine! Put it down!"

Four other men stepped out of the shadows. They wore white t-shirts and pants, clothing that hinted at powerful muscles hiding beneath. Their radiant faces and piercing blue eyes scanned the room for only a moment, before they stepped toward the table.

The man in black hissed and backed away. "Leave him alone... he's mine!"

The four men took positions around William, ignoring the man in black.

The man drifted back to the shadows from which he emerged, his face pale and twisted with hate. "You can't do this! He's supposed to be mine!"

As the man in black disappeared, William slid out of his chair to his knees...

Praying.

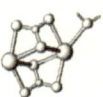

She looked at the pool sightlessly for some minutes, understanding now that when people desired to kill themselves, it was really the plan of an invisible evil. It crossed Gizile's mind that each night before falling asleep the prayers of her friends protected her in much the same way as she had just observed. She had never thanked them. Her own selfishness had kept her so consumed with grief and anger, she never realized so many people still loved her.

Maybe she wasn't alone after all.

She turned to Master Tok, to find him watching her now instead of the clouds. "Thank you," she said. "I've been a selfish scylla, and I should have been shelled like one, too."

He grunted. "The pool, girl. It ices."

She turned her thoughts back to the pool, and watched a man open a book.

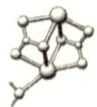

ears

P. A. Baines

"Look at their ears."

Carl stares down at the words on the page for a moment and chuckles quietly to himself. He glances around as if to share the joke with someone but he is alone. The shop is deserted apart from the severe-looking cashier pretending not to keep an eye on him over her horn-rimmed glasses. Dusty shelves crammed to overflowing lean towards him as if to share a secret. Outside, the rain persists and the alley is as empty as it was when he stumbled in a quarter of an hour earlier.

He flips to the book's cover. *The Path to Self Discovery*. A man's head is looking up towards some invisible star, his face obscured by a silver blue aura. The author's name sounds Indian. It hints at some deep, mystical knowledge.

"Look at people's ears and imagine how they would appear to someone who has never seen ears before. Soon you will only see ears."

Carl shrugs and replaces the book, in a gap between *Find Your True Being* and *Live the Blessed Life*. It is a tight fit and he has to wriggle it a little. He feels the cashier's eyes in the back of his head.

He checks his watch and realizes he only has a few minutes left before the end of his lunch break. The rain has let up but is still driving rivulets down the window. Someone scuttles past the door—raincoat collar pulled up high over ears.

149

"Look…"

Carl strolls along the aisle, his eyes roaming the sea of titles. Many have similar themes. The words "self", "love", "power" and "life" repeat more often than most. Some are new. Many look ancient. A vaguely musty smell teases his nostrils. At the back wall he comes to a section filled with titles about healing using everything from crystals and visualisation, to sounds and even colours. This leads into books about relationships, friendship, marriage, and one or two that make him look away with embarrassment. He hurries a little here, until he comes to a shelf with books on unsolved mysteries: the Yeti, the Loch Ness, pyramids, UFOs and aliens.

He reaches up, allowing his hand to touch the spines, and hesitates. He feels suddenly foolish.

As an actuary for a large insurance company he has little time for flights of fancy. His world revolves around numbers and formulas, odds and statistics, tables and charts. His days are filled with histograms, standard deviations, and risk assessments. Ordinarily he has no interest in such things as UFOs or aliens. It is a revelation to him that so much time and energy has been spent on things which are, to use a term he understands, outside his sample population.

He becomes aware that the rain has stopped and also that his break finished three minutes ago. The woman watches him leave. His polite smile is not returned.

Back at the office his mind returns to the real world, but his normally solid concentration is as slippery as an eel and he catches himself gazing out of the window more than once.

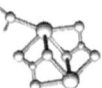

The next day at lunchtime Carl is the first out of the office. He has been distracted all morning and decides he needs fresh air. He heads to the park and takes the first available bench.

The sun bathes him in gentle warmth and he breathes deeply. Out on the lake, a family of swans probes the dark water for food. Beyond that a dog chases a ball as if it were the last thing on Earth. A slow but steady trickle of office workers invades the grass in a casual land-grab.

The soft pounding of rubber on gravel approaches and he turns to watch a young woman in a tracksuit and headband jog breathlessly past. Her ponytail and headphone wire bounce in unison to a barely-audible back-beat. Her hair is pulled up high on her head, revealing her …

"…ears."

Suddenly he becomes aware of just how strange her ears really are. Like fleshy pipes adorned with blobs of skin stuck onto the sides of her head. He stares at them—fascinated. They remind him of absurd pink mushrooms. Everything else about her is perfectly normal—except for those weird attachments.

He laughs out loud, which is something he never does. It is a snorty kind of laugh, bordering on a sneeze. It is the kind of sound you make when something is both funny and ridiculous at the same time.

He looks around to see if anyone else has noticed. Surely someone…An elderly couple approach—walking their dog—in the same direction as the jogger. He looks at them to see if they have noticed, but they are engrossed in their walk. They are both watching their dog sniffing at the verge. They watch it the way a young couple watches a toddler. Suddenly he notices the man's ears. They are bigger than the jogger's with more flesh at the end of the tube. The man's white hair and bald patch emphasise their pinkness and Carl lets out a small snicker.

They turn and glare at him and he looks away, all hot in the face. As they stalk off he cannot help but stare some more. They are truly grotesque.

At the next bench a serious-looking man is reading the newspaper. Immaculately dressed in suit and tie—his hair freshly cut. His leather suitcase sits at his feet, reflecting off his polished shoes. The paper rustles in his hands—a broadsheet—as he turns the page. It is the *Financial Times*. Must be a banker. Or a stockbroker. Looks like he drives a big executive car. Probably lives in an up-market part of the city. Possibly a house in the country.

In his mind's eye, Carl plots this man on a distribution curve. Expensive house and car. Secure neighbourhood. State of the art burglar alarm.

The man turns away, placing the newspaper sideways on the bench, looking down as he shifts his weight onto one buttock.

They are small, with narrow pipes and skinny lobules. Skin pale against his black hair…

"No!"

Carl forces himself to look away. This is ridiculous. He returns to his office, not stopping off for his usual sandwich. He avoids looking at people, and closes the blinds in his room.

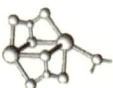

In Carl's dream, he is in a crowd. Rain is tumbling onto his shoulders from the umbrellas of those around him. He turns to find a way out but he is hemmed in. He looks around but cannot see their faces. All are dressed the same. Black raincoats. Black umbrellas. He looks up. He has no umbrella; the only one who has no umbrella. The rain spatters his face and he blinks at the dark sky. He wipes his face with the back of his hand.

He looks around but they all have their backs turned. His muffled calls go unnoticed. They cannot hear him even though they have such big...

...ears as big as his hand. Huge fleshy mounds that dominate the sides of their heads, hanging down onto their shoulders. Ears as big as buckets, pushing back and around until the stalks touch and he cannot see their heads anymore. Until the two are joined into one enormous ear.

He screams at them but they cannot hear. He screams until he finds himself upright, awake in his bed, the sweat trickling down his back.

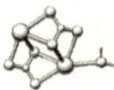

"It's their ears," he says. He sits with his head turned and his eyes averted. "It's all I can see."

"So, when did you start noticing...ears?"

The voice is calm. The voice is patient. The voice comes from years of practice. It is designed to soothe raw and exposed nerves. It belongs to a face Carl only dared to look at for the briefest of moments as he came in. In case he should see...

"Two days ago. I read something in a book. It started out as a joke."

The wall is adorned with certificates. Diplomas. Degrees. A doctorate in psychiatry. A photograph of a happy family. All smiles in front of a cloudy, blue background. No mental health problems in that picture. Just

152

ears.

Carl whimpers and forces himself to look away.

"It seems to me you have developed a fixation. You say you are an actuary?"

"Yes."

"And you describe yourself as something of a perfectionist?"

"Yes. I guess I would."

The office is filled with plants and ornaments. It looks like an office you might find in someone's home. There is a lot of wood. The colours are warm.

"Would you say you are a stickler for detail?"

"I don't understand."

"Do you get upset over small things?"

"Well yes, I suppose I do. But I'm not obsessive if that's what you're driving at. At least I don't think I am."

The shapes in the office are soft and smooth. The ornaments are tasteful. No sharp edges anywhere. The one on the table under the window is a mahogany carving. It is a stylised rendition of a woman and child. The shapes are vague, the curves exaggerated. Yet it is still possible—if you look closely enough—to make out what looks like…

"Please, no!"

"I'm going to prescribe some medication. Take this slip to the receptionist. She will give you the relevant forms. I want to see you again next week."

Carl leans towards the doctor to take the slip. He keeps his head lowered to avoid looking. He forces himself to stare at the polished oak coffee table that separates them—so polished he can see his own reflection as clearly as if he were looking into a mirror. His and that of the doctor. The doctor who has the biggest ears he has ever seen.

He lets out a short, sharp scream and jumps back into the chair. The doctor's ears are enormous. Even from the front they stick out like slabs of beef.

"Now calm down," the doctor says, leaning closer. "There's no need to get upset."

"No." Carl stares at the doctor with wide eyes. "Don't come near me."

But it is not just the ears. It is also the nose that now fills Carl with repulsion. The thing just sits on the man's face, pointing at Carl like a fleshy accuser, above lips. Lips like rotten hamburgers smacking open and closed as he makes that awful sound. All the time watching him with bulbous, bug eyes.

"Assistance please," the doctor calls into an intercom.

"No. Don't come near me," Carl cries, crawling backwards as the doctor approaches with fat, puffy fingers clawing towards him.

Then the door opens and three orderlies appear. They too have the same horrendous features. Hamburger lips smack in unison as they approach. One has a syringe.

"Please stay calm. We just need to give something to help you relax."

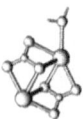

In his dream, Carl is in a crowd. It is the same crowd as in his last dream. Same umbrellas. Same coats. He is alone without his umbrella and the rain pours onto his shoulders. He blinks into the rain and feels the cool water against his skin.

He wipes his eyes dry and looks around. This time they are looking at him. Their ears, nose, lips and eyes are monstrous caricatures and he no longer recognises them as human. They shuffle towards him, squawking and screeching in some maddening alien tongue, their hamburger lips slapping open and closed.

He pulls back, but they are too solid. They close in on him, crushing the breath from his lungs.

Their fingers touch his face. Spindly claws grope his cheeks and pull his hair.

He tries to scream but he cannot. He tries to breathe in but his chest will not expand. The world swims before his eyes.

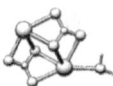

Carl wakes slowly, rising through the haze like a swimmer towards the sun. There are shapes and sounds all around him. He recognises voices.

Normal voices.

"He's coming around, look."

There are only vague shapes in front of his eyes. Colours blurred into each other.

"Hello? Are you all right?"

The shapes become a pinkish oval with smaller black objects inside. The black objects move in time to the voice.

"Don't worry friend. You'll be fine."

The shapes become eyes and lips. Carl is relieved to see that they look like normal lips and eyes.

"Here he comes. Back to the real world, eh?"

A face comes into focus. It peers closely, like a child examining a bug. The eyes are blue and clear. The lips normal. The nose looks like a nose. And the ears…

…the ears are normal! They don't stand out, or stick out, or look even remotely odd.

"Hi there. You back with us now?"

"What…what happened? I remember a needle."

"You're with friends now. I'm Luke."

"Where am I? And how did I get here?"

Carl tries to move but he feels restricted and it is still hard to breathe. For a second the nightmare sensation of being trapped returns. He realises that he is wearing a coat of some sort, but his arms are tied to his sides.

"A straitjacket? Why am I wearing a straitjacket?"

"We all get them here," Luke says. "Part of the uniform I'm afraid."

Carl notices that Luke is also wearing a straitjacket. There are other people in the room. All are wearing the same. One or two smile at him from where they are sitting. Some are watching a television high up on the wall. Some are just sitting, staring at the windows. The windows all have bars.

"What's going on? Where am I? Where's my doctor?"

"He probably put you in here, mate."

"You don't understand. I'm not insane. I just had…"

"A fixation?"

There is a noise outside the door. The rattle of keys in the lock. The others in the room become agitated and they all turn to look.

Two men dressed in doctors' uniforms enter, pushing a trolley loaded with cups and bottles of pills. They make the same screeching noise from his nightmare. And they have the same dreadful features. Ears, nose, eyes and lips. Hamburger lips.

"What are those things?" Carl whimpers, recoiling in horror. "Who are they?"

Luke leans closer, as if to share a secret.

"Their ears. Just look at their ears."

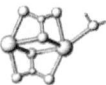

Gizile straightened up, thinking about what she had just witnessed. She heard Tok's gravel voice, "A whole new twist on being taken by the ears." Humor tinted his words.

She shot a look at her teacher. "It was not a funny vision. Obsession is a horrible thing, a great evil."

He gazed back innocently. "Is it? Perhaps then, you have not been taken by the ears enough!" Without a change of his normal, sour expression, he began to jitter slightly. Was he laughing at her?

She gave an unladylike snort and returned her attention to the pool—but not before noting his ears.

The ice began to form and she leaned in, ready to be sucked to another world. She saw a long-haired woman, young yet bent over. Gizile laughed despite herself. The woman's ears stuck out from between the strands.

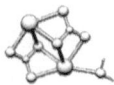

Lily's tale

Grace Bridges

A companion story to the novel *Legendary Space Pilgrims*

Lily Darcy. She's the crazy one. Haunted. That's what they all say. But do you know why she's crazy? Why she walks bent over, hair covering her face, avoiding the gazes of her colleagues?

I'll tell you. I'm the only one that knows, you see.

Lily has all her memories.

Yup. All the stinkin' things our mindwipes are meant to take from us. She's wired different or somethin', but she don't know cause she never told no one who might know why it is. At first, she was relieved. What kid doesn't dread their first wipe? But as the years progressed it became her curse. She lost her friends—their memories of her, anyway—with alarming regularity, yet she knew they all murmured about her "problem" when they heard the newest layer of gossip. There was always someone left unwiped to carry it on for another day.

Lily's crazy, yup. And Lily's me.

I figure this ought to be normal, somewhere on another world, Old Earth perhaps, or other colonies if there was any besides Monday.

Monday. What a joke, an excuse for a habitable planet. And what a sorry excuse for a so-called government, playing with their techno-toys and implants, taking children from their mothers, outlawing strong feelings, wiping the emotions and memories of those who transgress.

That's why they say Lily's crazy, too, cause she says all this is wrong. They don't see she only says so because the wipes don't rob her of her thoughts like they do everyone else.

So Lily's alone. She talks to herself. Yeah, you. No one else understands. You're one crazy chick. And it ain't the red hair, no matter what they say.

Crazy, but not unstable. I mean, as far as that's possible when you're the odd one out. It'd be hard not to have some kinks when you're the only one without 'em to start with, know what I mean?

Consequences of my ability mean I remember everything, nearly my whole life long. Not my mother; she only had me for a few hundred days. But my education, learning to read, hearing how emotions are bad, then deployment to the agricultural sector X and the oat division X9. Here, everyone picks oats.

What? What's that you're asking? Do I remember the mindwipes themselves?

I remember, and I quake.

A travel pod takes you far, far up into the sky, beyond the edge of space, to a huge round structure where thousands of Mondayites are found at any time of the day or night. The trip there takes hours, so that the air in the pod grows stale and you get lightheaded. Then the tube spits you out into a round room and you're on this table. A robot arm slaps a drug patch on your neck. There are voices, repetitive, calming for some, hypnotic for sure, the things they say are designed to make you fear emotion and deny it even though you don't want to. They tell me I am nothing, worthless, meaningless, and they say over and over that I now know nothing of my prior emotions. I guess it would work if the hypnosis and drugs didn't malfunction on me.

Yet when it's finally over and I'm sent on the heart-stopping pod ride back down to the surface, I still know everything I knew before. Feel it, too, although I shake in my boots from the ordeal. That's not what the Baxters intended—they want to reduce me to nothing and send me back to work as a productive citizen. So I make sure I am. Who knows what they might do to me if they found out?

I tell you, though, it's so painful to watch my friends be wiped again and again. Especially Caitlin and Mario. In a more perfect world, they would have been meant to be together. Here, they keep falling for each other all over again after each wipe. For a long time I thought to myself, it'd be over for sure if they were both taken at once.

I saw it coming a few days earlier, right after Mario's last wipe. The guy was besotted even before he knew there'd been something going on before he forgot it. They both tried hard to stamp out their feelings, but it was no use. I watched in as much horror as I could allow myself as she told him she loved him, and her emo-reader beeped up a racket. Mario tried to save her, but he couldn't.

Then the real weird thing happened. He'd been into reciting some poetry lately, and that's what he did now. His reader goes off too, and next thing you know, he's off for wiping as well.

You know what the strangest thing is? I never saw the like in all my days. Neither one ever came back. New kids took their places in the harvesting line, and that was that. Their friend Irina went around with a big frown on, but I didn't dare talk to her about it—she's very emotional and would be wiped in three minutes flat. Mario's dorm buddy Aaron looked so shocked too, and I thought I'd better leave well alone, though I did catch some intense glances from him. Wonder what he's been thinking about.

I'm not sure how many days later it was. I'd had another mindwipe in the meantime, you see—not that I lost any memory, but it sure rattled me up, like they always do. In any case, Irina vanished as well. It was the darndest thing. She wasn't taken from the field, or we'd have seen it. Must have been sucked out of her quarters—the very worst way to go. A place that ought to be safe, but even in private you can be snatched away and tortured.

Anyway, here I am, all alone, as always. Watching, ever watching, for the return of my friends, though the probability is fading fast. Aaron tried to remember the poetry Mario got so crazy on, and he told me a few snatches of it as we sat in the courtyard after dinner. Something about listening to a Voice, and a whole lot of weird instructions about obeying, and loyalty, and truth. Very strange stuff. But it does make me feel good, and I can't explain why—it's as if, even in this pitiful, grey world, there might be a reason to hope.

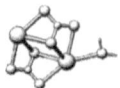

Did you see what happened there today, Lily? Do you remember it? Because you should. It changes everything.

You were sad. Not just a little bit, either. You were about to get mindwiped, and you knew it because the chip in your neck was beeping like crazy. You missed Caitlin and Mario and Irina who were really gone, and all the others whose bodies remained but their memories were gone. Face it, chick, you were having a cry—a sure recipe for a trip you didn't want.

The other harvesters glanced at you, and those nearest moved away so they wouldn't get taken by accident. That never actually happens, but you understand. Oat suction was still running, so you had a little more time before your ride.

Then, under your hair, out of the corner of your eye, you saw someone approaching. You started up and found you were looking into Aaron's face.

"What are you doing, cowboy? Get away while there's still time!" you splutter.

He steps nearer. "Listen to me," he says, "l-listen. Can you d-do that for me? Focus on the words."

You shrug, more from shoulder-heaving sobs than anything else, but he takes it as his cue to go on.

"Listen to me. I must be first. Th-that's what the Voice said."

"Mario's Voice." A shudder of some long-forgotten feeling traces your spine.

Aaron nodded. "And he said don't confuse him with anyone else, and don't speak carelessly about him."

Your beeping calms as you laugh suddenly. "How do you know it's a him?"

"I don't. Mario always called him him."

"What else did he say, then?" You've both gotten yourselves left behind the harvesting line. There might be trouble later.

"Be quiet and listen if you want to hear him speak."

"He's repeating himself."

"It's poetry. He's allowed."

"Go on."

"This bit's complicated. He wants us to do what he says, and also what other people say, people he's gonna send. I think that's what it was."

You smile at last. "I remember the next bit. Life is worthy, so live like it."

"Yeah!" Aaron's grin widens. "Be loyal, not nasty, respect people and tell the truth."

Together the two of you spoke the final patched-up line. "Don't want anything if you haven't got it, because I'll make sure you get what you need."

The silence is deafening. Your beeping has stopped.

"Woah." Aaron's happy.

You both rush to catch up with the others. They stare openly. Fair enough. Anyone beeping like you were a moment ago ought to be anywhere but here right now.

So you remember that, Lily girl. And remember those words. They saved you! That's one unusual poem all right.

Why, thank you.

Who said that? I'm busy talking with myself here.

Listen to me—I must be first.

Oh. It's you. Mario's Voice. Hey, you here, quit shaking. I know you're scared, Lily, but come on. Is this for real?

Do not confuse me with another, and do not speak carelessly of me. I want to be your Voice too.

Are you laughing at me?

Be still and listen, and I will speak. I'm just glad to be with you.

Woah. Why?

Monday's going to be free, and you're going to help me. Obey what I ask, and the Pathfinders I will send you. Respect what belongs to another.

Just like that, huh?

Treat life in a manner worthy of me. Esteem loyalty and do not give in to bent desires. So you want to hear how the rest of it really goes?

You tease. Go on then.

Speak the truth at all times, and do not wish for anything I do not give you, for I will give everything you need.

Are we going somewhere?

Not like Mario and Caitlin did, but yes, there is a journey ahead.

Are they all right? Where did you take them?

Yes. You'll see.

Quit that shaking, girl. Uh…It's strange, you know, talking to Lily when she knows you're listening.

So go ahead and talk to me instead. I'm here.

162

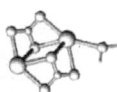

Gizile came to herself with a jerk when an unexpected wave crashed the ice away. Did others hear the same still, quiet voice she did? A warmth began to grow in her chest. It spread, chasing the chill from her body. Was he real, then? Could he care about *her?* Maybe everything she thought, all her anger toward him was…wrong. Maybe.

She smiled as she waited for the next incoming wave. When the water froze, she saw nothing. Only white. She leaned forward and strained her eyes. Yes. The vision was there. The white was a room.

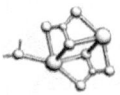

gravity

Travis Perry

He awoke to a room with white walls and ceiling, an off-white floor and an off-white frame on the single narrow window, feeling incredibly heavy, lying on a vaguely familiar spongy surface. His mind scurried to remember who he was and why he was there, but his thoughts were heavy, and no answers came.

A man wearing gray moved toward him through a blue-framed doorway, arms bare halfway up with impossibly massive biceps.

The muscular man pushed something toward him; it had the shape of a chair, but not quite. The giant leaned in close, his formidable bulk a menace. The massive stranger wasn't familiar to him, still, based on size alone, he felt a panic building that gripped him in his chest and throat.

Get away, he screamed inside, but his voice came out as a hoarse croak. He tried to move himself away but his head was too heavy to lift. He swiped his hands at the big man, aiming at his face, but the other just casually brushed the hands aside, reached for him, lifted him effortlessly and moved him with surprising gentleness into the chair. Even as he tried to gouge the giant's eyes out, he dully perceived that the other had said something to him in a calm, quiet voice.

Sitting upright, he could hold up his head, but it took a great effort. *I'm a prisoner here,* he realized. His memories were hazy, but he definitely recalled not wanting to be there and being moved and poked and prodded against

164

his will. He intuitively knew what the man said would help him understand what was happening to him, so he strained to bring the words back to mind.

An unrelated word came to him unexpectedly. *Gravity.* There was a lot of gravity there. A powerful flash of insight swept over him. *It explains so much.* The bulk of the stranger, his own leaden weakness, his imprisonment, even his difficulty thinking somehow fit with him being a prisoner on a high gravity world. *Did they win the war? Have I told what I know? What have they done to my memory?* What he could have told, what it was he knew, or who was warring, right then he couldn't recall, but he did know that he had written about these things, about alien worlds, interstellar wars, and gravity. Especially about gravity.

The big stranger took him through a white hall lined with blue doors, moving smoothly, as if floating. *Beyond these doors, no doubt, are other prisoners.* He heard someone shouting, a woman's voice, terrified, screaming, "Help me! Help me!"

As he moved, a jumble of images played through his mind, images of starships firing and aliens with pointed ears and humans struggling to survive against dark enemies and men with dark thoughts adapted to strange worlds, men with massive muscles striding smoothly through crushing waves of gravity. And he lay helpless against his own weight, moving forward, down a hall, going where he knew not.

At the end of the hall was a fairly large room full of people seated at semicircular tables. The tables reminded him of the crescent moon. *The moon.* He could see the moon in his mind, brilliant-white and shiny. The memory was so clear and strong that its beauty dazzled him.

He found himself sitting at the outside edge of a roundish table, wondering how he got there, his hands resting on its smooth surface. There were people next to him, all strangers, sitting on the edge of the moon, like him. On the inside curve of the table sat just one person, a woman in grayish clothing. She was petite, not muscular. *Somehow that isn't right, she shouldn't be so small,* he thought.

And then, *Wasn't I thinking something, just a bit ago? Something having to do with size or weight or something? Or was it something to do with the moon?*

The woman set an item in front of him. She held a small object up to his mouth and spoke to him. He looked right at the object but didn't understand until he smelled it that it was food. *That is how they are doing it.*

That is how they have ruined my mind. It's something in the food!

"Get that poison away from me," he growled. *I will not eat.*

The woman spoke to him in a soft voice and smiled. She said he needed to keep up his strength, and that he understood, for he felt so weak. He ate some. She told him how well he was doing that day. He thought about the moon, about children, about stars, about writing, about starships perched on the verge of attack, about food, and about gravity. *My thoughts are like a wind, gusting and changing directions.*

After some time, he didn't know how long, the woman in front of him took away the thing she had set on the flat thing where his hands were. A large muscular man, larger than any he could ever remember seeing, came to him. He moved him toward a hallway. On the side of the hall, on the wall, he saw a sign as he moved in. "Alzheimer ward," it said.

I wonder what that means.

As the burly orderly pushed him in his wheelchair down the hall with white walls and blue doors toward his room in the nursing home, he noticed how heavy he felt in the chair.

"Gravity," he muttered out loud. "There's a lot of gravity here."

A wave destroyed the ice and washed the pieces away.

Tok broke his silence. "Hmph. If you're not happy with the world, invent your own. That works."

"And if that person can't help himself?" Gizile asked.

"Can't is true for some…but what if they won't?"

"If a person has the ability to change a world they are unhappy with, then they should do so. Not pretend that it is what it is not."

Tok just grunted, but Gizile had the feeling the grunt meant more than she perceived, and that he was pleased with her answer. They fell silent once more as another wave broke.

the Field trip

P. A. Baines

Space holds its breath.

A spark glimmering like a diamond while, all around it, the stars twist and distort.

If sound could travel through space it would be a deafening shriek of tearing metal, the pounding of a million drums, a billion nails drawn down a blackboard, or a trillion worlds colliding.

Mercifully, there is no sound.

Then a craft, small and shiny as a brilliant drop of water, hovers as if it has always been there. Its two occupants sit for a moment, trapped in the folds of space and time, caught in a freeze-frame of wide-eyed surprise.

The clock on the dashboard hesitates then carefully, slowly, almost painfully, squeezes itself onto the next pulse like glue through a tube.

The taller of the two occupants blinks. He still has a wide-eyed look etched on his face. This may be due to shock or it may be his normal expression. It is hard to tell.

His smaller companion finishes scratching his nose, an act he started a billion light years away. By the time evidence of this event reaches their home planet at normal light speeds there will be no one there to witness it. Indeed, there will be no planet, although this does not bother him in the slightest, mainly because he does not understand it. He would not understand the idea of folding space if it were explained to him half a dozen times very slowly using diagrams and the latest in multimedia. Which it was.

His finger hovers close to his nasal cavity but he remembers that he is not alone.

The taller points through the windscreen.

A planet. A blue orb with swirls of white, punctuated by brown patches of land surrounded by water.

"Earth."

The smaller stares, his nasal cavity forgotten, his finger now extended towards the jewel floating before them.

"Earth."

The taller taps a button on the console. Text fills the screen.

A dismembered voice starts the lesson in the slow, measured tones of a teacher who understands the vast limitations of his students.

Spoob lunanga Stoonasweswe…

(translated)

This is planet Stoonasweswe. The inhabitants call it Earth. It is in the Doonago galaxy, known locally as the Milky Way. It is the third planet from their star called the Sun. Their system consists of thirteen planets, four of which they have not yet discovered. Circumference at the equator is 24,901.55 miles. Diameter at the equator is 7,926.28 miles. Average distance from Earth to the Sun is 93,020,000 miles. They have one satellite they call The Moon. Highest point on the Earth's crust is the volcano Chimborazo in Ecuador at 20,561 feet above sea level. Lowest point on the Earth's crust is Challenger Deep, Mariana Trench in the Western Pacific Ocean at 35,840 feet below sea level. Dominant species is humanoid, known as homo sapiens.

A picture of a naked human male appears on the screen. The two recoil in disgust. The taller spills some of his drink on the control panel. There is a spark and a hiss. The picture on the screen judders, then settles.

Humans are rated the fourteenth most intelligent species on the planet but they are by far the most aggressive. The most intelligent species is the sloth, although they lack the energy to do anything useful. Next are elephants, dolphins, whales, crows, cats and certain molluscs. Humans have divided the planet into one hundred and ninety-five countries, apparently at random. A number of these countries are in dispute. Humans enjoy watching television, eating, fighting, singing, and sleeping. The average human sleeps for eight hours a day, which explains why they have yet to understand such simple concepts as how the universe began.

The two snicker. The smaller says "poonikuk" which roughly translates as "idiots". The screen judders again. Text moves shakily up and down for a moment, and stops.

Humans are, however, in spite of their obvious stupidity, capable of amazing feats. Their art is known throughout the universe for its naive charm. Their music, particularly, soul, is enjoyed as far away as Sque on the outer edge of the universe where James Brown is considered something of a deity.

Perhaps their greatest achievement, however, is finding a solution to the impending ice age that strikes their planet every twenty thousand years. By spewing carbon dioxide into the atmosphere they have raised the temperature just enough to avoid certain doom. Many suggest that this was sheer coincidence and that humans had no idea of the approaching catastrophe, but few believe that any species can be that ignorant. This ends the lesson on Earth.

The text on the screen vanishes. The two blink.

Another line appears. It judders twice. Words flash on and off and on again. They both read the line very carefully, mouthing the words. The taller looks to the smaller who blinks back at him. The taller shrugs and presses a small red button on the corner of the console.

In front of the craft a green light appears. It is as bright as a small star. It spins, slowly at first, then faster and faster until it is a blinding blur. Space holds its breath for the second time that day. The two blink. The light explodes with furious energy as it flies towards the earth like a bullet. The two gasp.

The light fades from view. A moment later there is a silence inside the silence. They can hear nothing, but even that seems to have gone. They hold their breath.

The planet in front of them, Earth, Stoonasweswe, the beautiful blue planet with wispy streaks of water vapour…

Shatters.

Like a huge ball of the most delicate glass tapped by a hammer, it instantly turns into countless tiny fragments, each no bigger than a grape.

The two turn to each other with wide eyes.

"Ebooooola."

("Cooool").

The screen judders again. The sentence flashes off and on. Words appear and disappear. They both lean forward and read. It is the same sentence as before, only it isn't. The first time they read it, it said:

Remember: observe not, destroy.

This time the comma has moved. This time it says:

Remember: observe, not destroy.

They look at each other again and blink.

"Oosha."

("Oops").

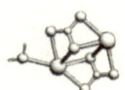

Gizile shook her head. "All those people…" She glanced at her teacher. "Are these visions real? Do they tell of actual events?"

He laughed, but then became grave as he stared into the pool. "I do not know if they are real. But they are truth to the watcher. They are lessons."

Gizile turned back to the pool and watched the last of the shattered ice wash away. "Are these visions truth for me then?"

He was silent a moment as the next wave washed in. "They are what you must learn."

The water crackled as it froze again. "And what was I to learn from watching a world destroyed?"

He grunted and shook his head. "Child, child."

She took a deep breath and watched the next vision come into focus. What she saw took her breath away. A strange beast…attacking a man.

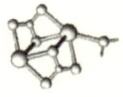

your average ordinary alien

Adam Graham

The Malnarian sank its teeth into the human's well-tanned back. Blood spurted all over the purple rocks and green sand. An energy beam zapped the Malnarian in the back. It turned. Yornac stood in his priestly robe. "Leave him alone in the name of peace!"

Kirk leaned forward in his ice blue chair. *Enough with the talk, Yornac. Zap that bad boy.*

The Malnarian dropped the human and approached Yornac.

Yornac raised his hands. "You leave me no choice. By the power of the seven moons of Galvark, you will die."

The Malnarian shrieked as its body decomposed. Yornac ran towards the human. "No, please, by all that is—"

An Earth woman about a meter and a half tall and of medium build blocked Kirk's view. The spiky-haired vixen hit a button and the HD plasma television went black.

Recognition hit Kirk. He glared up at Terry. "What are you doing, woman? I need to find out what happened with Yornac."

Terry rolled her eyes. "Relax. You Tivoed it." She took a breath. "Kirk, I don't know how to say this. So I guess I'll just—I'm leaving." Tears sparkled in her eyes.

Oh no. His sustenance was being cut off. And worse, who would keep his bed warm on cold winter nights?

He stood and put his arms around her. "Baby, I'm sorry. I know it's been a bit of a cold spell since I got laid off."

Terry shook him off. "It's been four years since you were laid off, and all you've done is live off me. You've spent all your time and money at sci-fi conventions. Even if you looked for a job, you couldn't find one after you changed your name."

Kirk grunted, plopping on the ice blue couch. She didn't think he was a loser back when he was earning $80,000 a year working for a dot com. She'd loved riding in his BMW and sitting in the hot tub of his plush apartment. Back then, it was all "you're so funny and smart." Now, after a short time out of work, she thought he was a bum. "Look, taking the name Kirk Picard Skywalker won't stop anyone from hiring me. Come on, something's changed."

Terry paced past Kirk's collection of Star Wars posters. "It's the church I'm going to."

Kirk jumped up. "I knew it! Those religious fanatics have nothing better to do than disrupt our happy home."

Terry bit her lip. "You said you were going to marry me when you moved in."

"I will. Just give me more time. A former coworker in Japan e-mailed me a prospect."

"Your old coworkers in Japan are twenty-something losers who stay in their pajamas all day and live in their parents' basements."

Kirk slammed his hand on his custom-made Stargate SG-1 coffee table. "Their garages!"

Terry rolled her eyes.

Kirk heaved a sigh. "Look, why believe this tripe about living in sin? All it has brought the world is suffering. When people let go of religion and embrace rationality, mankind will reach the stars and become gods."

Terry gave Kirk a peck on the cheek, like she might give her brother. She ran her hand across his uniform shirt, touching the Star Fleet logo. "Kirk, that's a nice story, but it's not true. I can't live like this anymore. I've got to go." Terry strode toward the door.

What would he do without real human contact? Sure, she'd been the ice princess for the past few months, thanks to the Church, but as long as she stayed, he had a shot. He glanced up at the model UFO hanging from the ceiling "The Bible and science fiction don't have to be contradictory.

Ezekiel saw a UFO, and do you really think Jonah was swallowed by a whale? No, classic case of deep-sea alien abduction."

Terry opened the door, but turned around. "I'm not even to that part of the Bible yet. Goodbye."

"But wait!" Kirk spied the Star Wars ships and a Klingon bird of prey hanging above the television. "You're my Princess Leia! I'm a Klingon and you're a female Klingon."

Terry closed the door behind her. Kirk plopped on the couch. How was he going to pay the rent? This must be why she'd had him re-sign the lease in his name alone last month. Eight hundred dollars in five weeks. How was he going to come up with that?

He looked up at the life-sized, autographed Luke Skywalker action figure standing by the closet. Selling it would pay the rent. No, that would be joining the Dark Side.

Kirk cried, "I'll never join you!"

If he sold his collection, what would he tell the guys over at the Sci-Fi message boards? How could he live it down?

Did they have enough left on the credit card to pay the rent? Oh great—that ungrateful wench had probably closed the credit card, too.

Maybe he could get a job. McDonald's was hiring. They were always hiring. But no, he couldn't work at McDonald's. That would debase him. He hadn't gotten a computer science degree to flip burgers. Still, a guy had to eat, until They came.

He looked out the window. A star streaked through the night sky. It was silly to wish upon a star, but he'd try it one more time. "Star light, star bright, I have an odd wish for you tonight. An ultra-fundamentalist like Terry wouldn't understand, but I want to be abducted by aliens."

He didn't want brought back, either. They had to let him join Them. He looked at his bulging belly. Hopefully, They weren't as strict about weight as the Air Force.

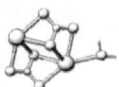

Kirk's eyelids fluttered. He lay on a cool metal table with his arms strapped down and a soft metal alien headband on his forehead. *Yes! This is*

more like it.

A green humanoid alien with an oversized, bald head faced the wall. He placed his six-fingered hands on the hips of his dark blue uniform.

The ceiling glowed pure white. A gray steel door reflected the gleaming room behind Kirk. A metal box on the back wall had flashing diodes blinking. Kirk grinned. "Woo-hoo!"

The alien turned around and sighed. His round, orange eyes focused on Kirk. "Accursed fecal matter. The anesthetic should have lasted two yorlans longer."

Kirk gasped. "You speak English?"

"Of course. We have Coca-Cola, too, and we have to learn English to deal with the Americans. They're taking over the universe."

So that was what the government was hiding. Kirk arched his eyebrow. "Really?"

The alien tilted back his head and chortled. "Humans are so gullible. The device around your head allows you to understand any spoken language."

"I could've used this in French class. Now what?"

"With most humans who wake up, I have to sedate them and do a memory wipe. But, with you, it won't be necessary."

Kirk smiled. "You see in me a kindred spirit with whom you can share the secrets of the universe? Cool."

"No. I saw your apartment. No one would believe you."

"Oh." Kirk paused. "So how far do you live from here?"

"About twenty Earth meters."

"Huh?"

"Oh, you mean how far is my home world? It is located in the Marchovias Galaxy, millions of light years from here."

A light blinked on the wall next to the reflective steel door. The alien glanced towards the light. "Please remain motionless."

A metal claw extended out of the wall and zoomed towards Kirk's face. Kirk screamed. The device grabbed his nose.

Kirk cried in a nasally voice, "No, I don't want to die!"

The alien growled. "Will you stop it! You're not going to die."

The device yanked out one of his nose hairs. Kirk yelped. The device released his nose and retracted. The alien put the hair in a round transparent case and placed it on a table. "It will be just a few yemnars while we analyze it."

"Why did you do that?" asked Kirk.

"A biological scan detected a flaw in two percent of the human population of your industrialized countries. Due to exposure to electromagnetic waves in recent years, the cellular structure of these humans has weakened. Our analysis indicates these humans will begin to break down genetically within ten years."

"What will that mean?"

The alien leaned against the wall. "Their cells will drift apart. In theory, it could cause an atomic reaction, but they would die before it reached that point."

Uh-oh. That was what he got for using the computer twenty hours straight. "Do I have it?"

"We don't know yet. That's why we're running the test on your nasal hair. We're close to coming up with a digestible cure that should eliminate the disease before it actually develops. Your governments will place it in your water supplies. The disease will be cured before anyone knows they have it. One of your computer makers sent out a software patch that changes the power settings to limit the damage."

"Whoa. So you're working with the government and the computer industry?"

"Of course. The computer companies sent us a hundred thousand bushels of hemp. They know what type of lawsuits this will cause if we fail."

Wait a second. "You're getting paid for this?"

"Yes. Hemp is a valuable product we use in construction on my world. When we return home, we'll sell it to the building industry, who'll sell it to consumers."

What? Had he been captured by Ferengi? These cold-blooded capitalists would do anything for a buck. "And what would you do if we couldn't give you any materials that you needed?"

The alien licked the area above his mouth. "If you didn't have any materials we needed, you also wouldn't have been advanced enough to get yourself into this predicament."

"But you should be doing this for free!"

"Where do you volunteer?"

"Um, well…nowhere."

"Why should we? We're saving six million of your fellow Americans from splitting apart into tiny pieces, and we're just asking for plants. I think that's a fair exchange. Besides, it's very hard to put eleven children through college on volunteer work."

Didn't he get it? Where was the enlightenment? "Surely not every alien race is a bunch of capitalists out for profit."

The alien sat at the end of the table and pulled a small cube out of his pocket. A 3D image of a tiny red alien with green eyes appeared on top of the cube. "This is Kunichita. I give thirty qindels a month to help him. On his world, there's no money, no trade, no merchants, only a state that will take care of the citizens and serve as their benefactor while it seeks to build a perfect world."

"That sounds more like it!"

"If you like absolute poverty. That's how they live. Without the help of sponsors like me, Kunichita has no food, no nothing. All the well-intentioned drivel in the universe, and none of it can compare to the results of diligent hands working to build for themselves."

"Oh, come on. There has to be some advanced race that's not so greedy."

"Tell me. You have something on your planet called communism, don't you?"

"Yeah, the communists were portrayed in Star Trek II as Khan and his men. Though Reagan also referred to the communists by making a reference to Star Wars—"

"I care not for your games. Has this system ever made a people wealthy?"

A news image of the bread lines in Russia flashed by Kirk. "No."

"Then why would it work on another planet?"

"But what are you going to do with all that money?"

The alien looked at the cube of Kunichita. "I'll fly to his planet and make him my son."

"But you shouldn't interfere with another culture. Who are you to judge?"

"According to your own logic, who are you to judge me? What idiot would object to intervening when there's a poor little male without a father?" The alien ran his hand across his barren scalp. "You know what I really want to do? I'll be able to retire next year and spend more time helping the poor churches on my world."

"Wait, you have churches on your planet? But they're not Christian churches. They're like temples, right?"

"No. They're Christian churches."

Now this was too much. "Whoa. Jesus was born on Earth."

The alien turned his head sideways. "Yes, the Prophet Melnish had a vision of Christ. Many thought the Prophet Melnish was dead and placed him in a tomb. When the Prophet Melnish emerged from the tomb, we believed his message. Though mockers scorned us for centuries, the discovery of Earth has caused a slight relaxation in skepticism."

At a beep, a metal slide fell out of the wall. The alien got up and grabbed it. "Good news, you don't have the genetic flaw and are unlikely to ever develop it. Unfortunately, that makes you of limited use for our study, but we may find some useful anti-bodies in your blood sample."

No way did a species become this advanced without more than this. "Come on, you're holding out on me. Tell me the secrets of the universe."

The alien sat on a stool. "I'm so glad you asked. According to the Prophet Melnish, the secrets are as follows: One, serve God with all you have. Two, love your family and care for them. Three, work hard, labor with diligence, for the diligent hand shall prosper. Four, save ten percent of what you earn and give ten percent of what you earn and you shall be blessed. Five, rest one Zannon a Yavlock. For you, just rest one day a week. Six, eat moderately and exercise. Seven, aim for peace with all. Eight, be compassionate to the poor, the needy, and the stranger."

Kirk's jaw dropped. "That's it? I could have gotten that off a box of tea."

"Yes. Melnish Tea is delicious indeed and teaches the lessons that all creatures must learn to have a good life. Now, let me release your bands, and I'll take you back."

After the alien had released Kirk from the table, Kirk jumped up. "Wipe my memory!"

The alien blinked. "Excuse me? That's really unnecessary and could cause vomiting."

"You've ruined my life! I finally get to meet an alien, and you tell me that you're flying green WASPs."

The alien looked up. "There's no insect on the ship, I assure you."

Kirk grabbed the alien. "I want the blue pill! I don't want to remember this. I want hope there are better aliens out there. You're lying about them! The secrets of the universe can be found. You just don't want me to know them!"

A dart of pain shot through Kirk's body.

The alien shook his head. "I don't understand you, Kirk Skywalker. Why would you live in a fantasy world when you know the truth? But as you wish, I'll wipe your memory. I shall keep you in my prayers."

The room spun into darkness.

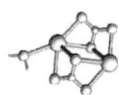

Kirk sat up in bed. The clock read eleven a.m. Man, he had to get up earlier if he wanted to find a job.

He padded to the kitchen and opened the fridge. Terry had left it almost full. He had enough food to last a couple weeks, but then what? He strode into the living room.

Life-sized Luke Skywalker smiled, with his light saber drawn. For some reason, it seemed less important this morning. If worst came to worst, he could sell it, but he had a lot more he could get rid of before he got to that point.

He swung open the front door, scooped the paper off the step, and brought it inside. He pulled out the comics and the TV guide and reached for a part of the paper he hadn't touched in years—the classifieds.

Maybe he'd take a look at them in the afternoon. Kirk plopped on the couch, picked up the remote, and turned on the television. A better world of space aliens and pirates emerged.

For some reason, he found it harder to believe than he did yesterday.

Tok rumbled a laugh. "All things age. But some grow up too...
eventually."

"They don't always become what you expect," Gizile said with a smile.

"Very good. You will be an excellent teacher someday."

Gizile turned to him. "I do not want to teach. I want to fight."

"And who will you fight?"

Gizile looked at the tidal pool, thinking of the previous vision. "I don't
know anymore. I've hated them for so long...but, they're just people, aren't
they, Master? They're like us."

"Some, yes."

"What should I do?"

Master Tok extended his arm to the pool. "Learn."

Gizile turned back to the crystallizing ice. "What is this? A strange
chariot flying through the heavens?"

"Learn," Tok said again.

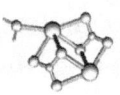

weapons of war

R. L. Copple

"Target in sight, Captain," announced the lead ship as they dropped out of inner-space. One-seater Shadowbird fighters flew in front, forming a V-shaped line. Captain Dan Roundtree, in his roomier Rioter fighter, held the quarterback position.

Their target, a twenty-kilometer, cigar-shaped cruiser of the Kulugans, glowed with starlight against a colorless backdrop.

Dan's ship boasted a new weapon dubbed the Acid Ray. Metal-eating acid extracted from the Caustic Nebula would ride a shield-penetrating plasma beam. Their cruiser wouldn't last an hour once hit. But he had to fly within twenty-five meters to deliver the knockout punch.

"Sir, the Kulugan fighters have exited the cruiser's bay, but are holding position behind it."

"I'm smelling a trap." He gripped his flight stick tighter. "But what exactly, I've no idea. Proceed as planned."

As they approached, the enemy cruiser emitted flashes along its port side. Waves rippled toward Dan's squadron, as if someone had thrown a rock into a pond. Dan realized too late that a strange new weapon raced toward them.

His heart skipped a beat. The greatest fear of man, the unknown, now flew at him. His last thought before impact: *One good secret weapon deserves another.*

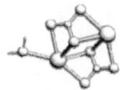

Dan awoke. His head pounded. He forced himself to focus on the viewer through the pain—a gray screen stared back. He pushed the button for the view port to open—nothing.

He sighed. *Great, their weapon drained the power. Not a bad idea. Powerless targets make for easy prey. But why am I still alive?*

Dan pulled a pole from an enclosure, which folded open to a crank. He struggled with the rarely-used device; the view port doors ground open. He sat and scanned the spinning stars.

There. He saw rays shooting around a large ship off in the distance. *Surely one of them will break off to tow me back.* Yet no one came to his aid. The fight receded into the stars.

He checked his oxygen level, luckily a mechanical dial. He had enough for two hours. Then it would be a slow, agonizing death.

After spinning through space for an hour, Dan arose and stared out the window. Rolling past the port, a cruiser emerged from the void.

That's the Kulugan cruiser. But how can that be? Have I come upon another battle? A squadron of Shadowbird fighters in a V-shape approach formation with a Rioter ship behind them dropped out of inner-space. This had to be the same battle—though it made no sense.

Dan figured the Kulugans would blast him. Yet, he drifted by the Kulugan cruiser, within the twenty-five meter range, ignored by everyone. He pulled the trigger, just in case. Nothing.

Dan saw his squadron approaching, except now he watched from a distance. The cruiser next to him flashed and the same rippling wave shot out toward the oncoming squadron. Is this another wave of fighters? Or... he didn't know if he should even think the thought.

As he watched, the wave reached the squadron and scattered the lead ships. As it hit the back ship, Dan's world went black.

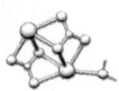

Dan awoke. His head pounded. He forced himself to focus on the viewer through the pain—a gray screen stared back. He paused. *What happened?* He glanced at the oxygen meter, and it showed just over two hours of air.

He scratched his head. So the rumors of the Kulugans' experimental dimension weapon were true. By throwing ships into an interphasic shift, they would lose their power. *But it sent me too far in and now I'm stuck in a repeating loop, invisible to their eyes. That's why no one came after me.*

He arose, engaged the crank and opened the view port doors. As before, he watched a dwindling fight. An hour later, the fight came back into view. Again, he flew in close to the cruiser. It shot the wave at the oncoming fighters and when it hit the back ship, he blacked out, then awoke and rode the same ride.

He cycled through ten trips. Each time he studied the scene and planned his attempt to escape the dimensional trap. On the eleventh pass, he initiated his plan.

He locked his helmet into place and disconnected the oxygen tank from its fittings. Using the manual release, he opened the hatch. A rush of air flew into space. He anchored the tank on the hull with the outlet pointing outward. When the Kulugan cruiser rotated under him, he fired the makeshift thruster. Several blasts of air later, he had adjusted course to collide with the Kulugan ship. Contact with an unaffected object should break him from the interphasic shift.

After closing the hatch, he attached the tank to his suit. The V-shaped line approached again, as did the battle. The cruiser filled the view port as he rotated around. He strapped himself into the chair and braced.

The two dimensions collided. Pops reverberated through the cabin like ripping bubble-wrap. Dan vibrated with his ship, and everything warped like a flag whipping in the wind. As the sensation passed, he heard metal scraping as his ship rolled across the cruiser.

Power returned. With expert hands, he stabilized the rolling ship, spun it around, and fired the Acid Ray. A tightly focused beam tore through the shields and bored a hole into their ship. A glowing red infestation widened.

He fired thrusters to escape. Cheers rolled over the com. "Sir, how did you—"

"No time now, Sergeant, just turn your tail and run. Now!" They complied without another word. A wave shot came from the cruiser, but it dissipated before it could reach the receding ships.

Dan scanned the cruiser; the hole enveloped a quarter of the ship. *Mission accomplished. But at what cost?* War has always been Hell, with no winners.

He peered into the view port of the ship next to him. His own face stared bug-eyed across the near vacuum at him.

"This won't be easy to explain to myself."

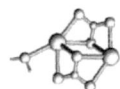

"No winners," Gizile said. Her mind drifted to her parents and the last time they were together.

"We won the battle," Tok said softly. "But the cost was high."

She wiped her eyes with the back of her hand. "I don't want to go on, Master. These truths are too difficult."

"Yes, they are."

"May we leave?"

"No. We are not done here."

"I don't think I can..."

"The pool, Gizile."

She turned back to the new ice. Lights. Explosions. War. "No more... please..."

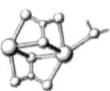

a small sacrifice

Mike Lynch

A flash of light discharged in the sky, followed by multiple explosions so strong, every window within a twenty-block radius of a place the locals called McDowell Park lay shattered.

Errant bolts of electricity darted out of columns of smoke as they rose above patches of lawn now covered in a thin layer of black. A soft breeze carried the ashen plumes away, leaving a lone figure—Kelsic 5—standing before a grove of box elder trees.

"Systems check," he said into his headset display, his weapon at the ready.

"Working at optimal preset limits," came the reply.

He looked down at his arm and checked the energy gauge affixed to his sleeve. Seventy-one teraquads of power left. Less than expected, but still enough to defeat his foe and leave him with a sufficient amount of energy for a successful jump off the planet.

The contrails from a distant airborne vehicle drew his attention upward. A blue sky set before a solitary moon. It had been a long time since he landed on a planet with a blue sky.

"Blue sky," he repeated into his headset. "What planet am I on?"

A series of clicks and beeps preceded the comset's response. "Accessing. Earth—third planet in the Sol System. Presently inhabited by an indigenous species known as humans. Global population now stands at—"

"Cease report." Humans. A survey study made of them some time back came to mind. Kelsic 5 made a three hundred and sixty-degree sweep of the area. Arboreal class life forms, terrestrial access ways, above ground dwelling units. *A most primitive and inferior species*, he concluded. *Not worthy of restrictive engagement protocols.*

The air around him stilled. Subtle at first, it grew in intensity, to the point where his polyphasic suit compensated for the pressure differential. His senses heightened with equal measure.

The white-hot bolt of an ion blast shot through the air, detonating a short distance away.

Kelsic 5 dove behind a stand of trees and returned fire. Multiple explosions from his pulse cannon lit up the sky, and then faded. Despite a modicum of protection offered by the thick foliage, he still felt exposed. Making a visual assessment of his surroundings, he opted for one of the nearby human transportation devices and crouched down behind it.

"Full directional scan," he said into his headset. "Locate enemy combatant." As the comset implemented the directive given it, the distinct sounds of screams came at him from multiple directions. Committed to his mission above all else, he ignored the distraction.

"Unable to locate combatant," his comset replied. "Zero energy signature readings detected within operational range."

Kelsic 5 slammed his fist into the side of the transportation device, causing a significant dent. "That Simeran must be using a reflective holo-field." He checked his energy readings. "Tricky to track, but not impossible."

"Non-sequitur. Please repeat command."

"Disregard."

He lifted his head just enough to view the open area. Where had his opponent hidden himself? Better the Simeran was invisible, he mused. They were the ugliest species in the galaxy anyway.

The air became still, like before. Kelsic 5 held his place and listened. Another ion blast came out of nowhere and slammed into his polyphasic suit, hurtling him into an adjacent transportation device. He brought up his weapon and fired blind. Several discharges struck a dwelling unit across from him, causing it to erupt in flames. He watched as a number of humans stumbled out of the smoke-filled entrance. Not much he could do for those creatures.

He jumped to his feet and took cover behind another vehicle. Kelsic 5 flicked a glance at his energy gauge. Sixty-one teraquads left. If he didn't terminate his opponent soon, he wouldn't have enough energy to make a successful jump off this wretched planet.

Kelsic 5 made another scan of the area, his attention drawn toward the plume of smoke as it drifted away. A physical principle came to mind. An object, even an invisible one, became visible when it passed through the particulate matter. Only one problem. How to get his opponent to pass through it?

He looked down at his pulse cannon and studied it a moment. *Perhaps with the right kind of bait.*

A quiet whimper sounded behind him. Kelsic 5 spun around and pointed his weapon at the source. It turned out to be a human cowering on the ground a short distance away. Dressed in strange, loose-fitting clothing, brown wavy hair partially covered the creature's face. *The female of their species*, he concluded. Though she didn't move a muscle, he sensed she was terrified beyond description. As he studied her more closely, he noticed a smaller human clutched in her arms.

"Please, don't hurt us," the female pleaded, her voice quivering.

He lowered his weapon until it rested against her temple.

All at once her eyes hardened, and she rose to her feet. "If you harm my child, so help me..." She pushed the muzzle of his pulse cannon off to one side and slowly backed away.

Curious, Kelsic 5 thought. He had the ability to disintegrate them both without a second thought, yet a protective need to save its offspring superseded her fears, even at the cost of her own life.

When another blast struck the dwelling unit behind him, the ensuing shock wave knocked him back a step. He cursed himself. His momentary lapse of judgment had almost gotten him killed.

Kelsic 5 brushed past the creature and headed back toward the area filled with rocks and trees, near the spot where he had first been fired upon. Black smoke continued billowing into the sky, just as he had hoped. He ducked down behind several large boulders not far from where he planned to lure in his prey. As he looked about, Kelsic 5 observed other humans carrying little ones away from the battlefield, using their own bodies to protect them.

He hadn't expected this. In his many encounters on other worlds, he had never once witnessed any member of such a primitive species willingly sacrifice their own lives to save their offspring. Such nobility only existed within his own kind, or so he had believed. And as such, the humans were worthy of a second chance.

Kelsic 5 accessed the informational database. "Amend assessment of human class life forms."

"Proceed when ready."

"Abort sanctioned elimination of planet. Contamination to culture is reversible."

Several clicks and bleeps sounded before the comset responded. "Amended assessment has been recorded."

"Good."

He peered past the boulder. A problem still remained, however. How to get the Simeran where he wanted him. Kelsic 5 brought up his weapon and studied it a moment before checking his energy gauge. Fifty-two teraquads remaining. If power levels dipped below fifty, he could be marooned on this planet for a very long time. Worse yet, the mission would be deemed a failure, and his superiors would almost certainly invalidate his recommendation. From what little he'd already seen in this species, he couldn't let that happen.

A difficult choice pressed down on Kelsic 5 like a great weight. If he jumped now, the Simeran would still be out there, committed to more destruction. If he didn't make the jump, his superiors would destroy the planet without hesitation. Either way, it didn't bode well for Earth.

When the power cell at the base of his pulse cannon caught his eye, a solution presented itself. Not the one he anticipated before his arrival, but it was the only outcome that made sense. "A small sacrifice," he whispered, and then jumped to his feet and headed straight for the plumes of smoke.

Ion fire erupted all around him, nipping at his feet after every step.

He took note of the direction each one came from until an arcing trajectory formed on the screen of his headset. Kelsic 5 counted to three, and then let off a volley of plasma bursts just to the right of the middle column of smoke. His shot hit dead center. The Simeran's mirror technology faltered, exposing him to the light of day.

Enraged he had been discovered, the gangly creature twice Kelsic 5's size came charging at him. The Simeran attempted to fire his weapon, but it must have been damaged by the explosion.

Kelsic 5 brought up his pulse cannon to finish him off, but he waited too long. The hulking creature tackled him, and the two soldiers became entangled in a fight for their lives. They rolled back and forth on the ground, grunting loudly and striking blows against the other in rapid succession.

Finally managing to pin his opponent with a full body lock, Kelsic 5 glimpsed his energy gauge showing itself in and around the Simeran's tentacles flailing about. It read forty-nine teraquads. Too late.

But it wasn't too late.

Kelsic 5 looked his enemy in his bulbous eyes and smiled. "This ends here and now." He flipped a switch on his weapon and set the power cells on overload.

A high-pitched whistle filled the air. It grew in intensity, until a flash of light discharged in the park, and the two were gone.

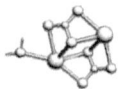

Gizile shuddered. The sobbing came unhindered. Suddenly there was a white cloth thrust before her face.

"No handkerchief again, I see. How many times have I told you preparation is everything, Gizile?" Tok rumbled.

She took the handkerchief, wiped her face and blew her nose, swallowed. "Tell me how my parents died."

"You are not ready."

She looked up at him, pleading with her eyes. Tok's face of stone softened and transformed into the face of weariness.

"Your father gave himself in much the same way as the vision…he held the pass long enough for me to bring the walls down. They fell, crushing the invading horde. Crushing him as well. He saved many lives."

"And my mother?"

Tok sighed. "She rushed in just after, before we could make sure everything was secure. She thought she could…rescue him. But there were a few of the enemy who survived. And the ring could not protect her from everything."

Gizile rubbed the ring on her finger again. Her mother's ring. She traced the intricately woven vines with her eyes.

"She was a great teacher," Tok said. "They both were. The war made fighters of everyone."

"Is that why you took me as a student?"

Tok firmed his lips. Then he nodded his head toward the pool. Gizile obeyed and turned back to the ice.

cLoser to home

Keven Newsome

The world revolved beneath my feet like a granite sphere on top of billowing water. Each land mass on that dark gray ball shone with the brilliance of a million stars, a tribute to Thomas Edison in a way few could ever appreciate. Long ago it would have been dark, but this galaxy of electric cities brought the world together in modern unity. Its beauty was surpassed only by the countless stars wrapping the Earth, looking with approval on the heroic human efforts at imitation.

I had often taken for granted the vastness of the galaxy. But now each miniscule grain of light shone with the intensity of the sun, an equal among its brothers. It was as if God had taken a handful of diamond dust and blown it onto a tapestry of black velvet. And looking upon his handiwork, he took another and still another, until there were more stars than velvet.

I saw the eastern seaboard roll over the horizon, adding its brilliance to the rest of the sparkling world. As more of the United States came into view, Houston emerged, its lights almost indistinguishable from those of Dallas, but the region easy to spot.

It was Home.

My family waited there. They waited patiently for me to return, but soon they would be told the truth…and it would crush them.

I thought of my son. His wild imagination always made my job more grandiose than I ever felt it to be. A "spaceman" he called me. At five he already wanted to follow in his father's footsteps, to traverse the stars and walk in space. He could get his chance…a chance to go further than I ever dreamed. By the time he gets to strap into a rocket, the frontier might be Mars.

But that would be something I would never see. I would never see him play baseball, or graduate from high school, or get married. I'd never see him become a man.

I stretched out my white-gloved hand toward my family. A tear leaked from my eye and formed a globlet, floating within my helmet.

I thought of my daughter. She would be a teenager soon, dating and searching for love. But she would always be daddy's little girl. I remembered when she was little and she would grab my arms and tug at me until I picked her up… the way she said, "I love you, Daddy," after kissing me softly. I hoped she would become the woman I knew she could be. I hoped she married someone who reminded her of me. I hoped she'd never forget.

Another tear floated away from my face, and I stretched my other arm toward home… just a little closer. The broken tether that had once kept me safely tied to the ship floated in my way. I grabbed it and jerked it backwards, not wanting reality to spoil my moment.

I thought of my wife… my best friend. I thought of the way she smiled when I came home, and how she held me tight. The way her golden hair splashed over her shoulders… the way she smelled of gardenias. Would she be all right? Would she be able to breathe when they gave her the news? Did she know already? I wanted so bad to take her in my arms and caress her back, to rub my cheek against hers… to tell her everything would be OK. But more than that, I wanted one last chance to tell her how much I love her. And I wanted to tell her to be happy… to learn to love again.

I strained my fingers and arms toward her, crying. Just a little closer, maybe she could hear me. The sound of my voice pressed against my ears, my short-range suit radio inadequate to carry it anywhere else.

But I couldn't hear my voice. All I could hear was theirs. The memories played through my mind like old home movies, reminding me of the blessings I had been given. The laughter and tears of a life… lived. I wished I had more time, but God had other plans.

I looked back at the broken shuttle, twisted and cleaved almost in two by a meteor. Every one was dead there, as I would soon be. Where were their families? What were their stories? Were they happy in life? Had they ever yearned for something more than what this life could give?

Had they ever met God? I should have asked.

A filament of orange outlined the horizon, like embers at the edge of a leaf. I closed my visor and waited as the glowing thread swelled and brightened, changing from orange to blue to white. After only a couple minutes, the sun emerged in a bright display of pure light unspoiled by the thick atmosphere below. The light washed over me like a warm blanket and my tears stopped, the floating water absorbed by the suit ventilation system.

Here I flew, two hundred and thirty miles above the slumbering surface, the only person in existence to witness this sunrise in this way. Its beauty could not be described. Its wonder could not be imagined. Only by the radiance of Heaven could it be surpassed.

I held my breath, stunned into stillness.

With the memories of my blessed life to accompany me, facing the most wondrous sight I had ever seen, it was only a matter of time until I moved from this life to the next. I pressed the throttle for my SAFER system and propelled myself toward the glowing sphere. My chest warmed with happiness. We all had to die, and I had been given the gift to pass from one wonder to an even greater wonder in a way no human had ever experienced. As I gained speed, I stretched my arms out toward the sun and stared into eternity, thankful that with each passing second I was closer to home.

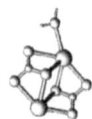

The wave obliterated the scene. There was much she didn't understand in the vision. Yet…yet, there was a joy also. Mourning, but an acceptance of what must be. Tears rolled down her cheeks unbidden. Her sobs echoed from the rock wall behind them. "Tok…"

The stoic teacher knelt and wrapped his arms around her.

"I miss them," she cried.

"So do I."

As they knelt together in the fading day, no more ice formed in the pool. Tok let her cry until the light had nearly extinguished. No words were needed. Not anymore. Tok took Gizile by the hand and brought her to her feet.

"Is there no more for the pool to teach?"

Tok shook his head. "Not so. There is no more for you to learn just now. Come." He turned away from the shore.

As they walked back up to the old keep, the first drops of rain began to pelt them.

"Tok?"

"Yes?"

"Will you teach me to be a teacher like my parents?"

The tall man answered without turning. "Yes, Gizile."

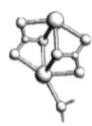

grace bridges

Grace Bridges has been in love with language her entire life. She's a semi-professional cat herder and also translates German and French. Indie publishing and freelance editing have been her focus for the past ten years, including 40+ titles in her Splashdown Books brand. She has written several novels in space opera, Irish cyberpunk, and in 2017 the EARTHCORE science mythology YA series set in New Zealand. Her short stories and non-fiction appear in various anthologies and online magazines.

http://www.gracebridges.kiwi

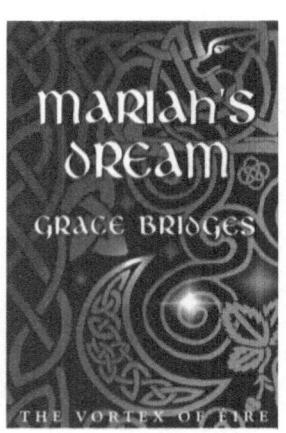

How far would you chase hope?
What if you could change the world?

The green has gone from Mariah's Ireland. Every garden and field that was once lush with crops is now lifeless muck. And yet Mariah holds one seed...the seed of hope.

Together with Liam, her staunchest supporter, Naomi the biologist, Deborah, whose son sold out to the Senate, and Peter the farm boy, she sets out to make Ireland green again. That is Mariah's hope. It is Mariah's dream. Mariah's dream will change everything.

Mariah's Dream—ISBN: 978-1927154-43-4

Anira doesn't like volcanoes very much, but still has to go along on a family trip to the geothermal wonderland surrounding the city of Rotorua, New Zealand. Around her forms an unlikely band of heroes, united by the strange and diverse abilities they gain from the area's earth-fed hotspots. They are about to find out the reason that goes deeper than DNA. All of them—and their supernatural backup—will be needed to outwit the unscrupulous developer bent on turning the whole town into a gambling strip.

Earthcore Book 1: RotoVegas—ISBN: 978-1927154-50-2

Fred Warren

Fred Warren hails from the merry old land of Kansas, and his short stories have appeared in a variety of online and print magazines, such as A Fly in Amber, Beyond Centauri, Every Day Fiction, Mindflights, and Residential Aliens.

You can find links to his other stories in print and online at his writing blog, http://frederation.wordpress.com.

Stan Marino needs a muse. He's written himself into a corner…again.

A shot of inspiration is all he needs to finish his story…where is he going to find it? What Stan doesn't know: Inspiration has found him, and it's about to take over his life. Ripped from reality, he must lead a band of lost souls in a life-or-death battle with a merciless enemy.

Stan has found his muse, but will he survive it?

The Muse—ISBN: 978-09864517-1-3   *The Seer*—ISBN: 978-1927154-15-1

Follow Fred through the twists and turns of twenty-two bizarre tales, where odd is common-place, little things make all the difference, and miracles are everywhere, if you know where to look.

Do the impossible. Change the future. Save the world.

All you need is one odd little miracle.

Odd Little Miracles—ISBN: 978-9876531-1-6

caprice hokstad

Caprice Hokstad spends most of her time dreaming up other worlds to live vicariously in. She lives in a mobile home in southern California, but regularly stares at her simulated aquarium screensaver. Her ultimate aspiration is to live in the first undersea colony, Atlantica, currently being built off the coast of Florida. She is assured they will have electricity and internet and that there will be room for her laptop, so she can continue to write. At that point, she may change her screensaver, but no promises.

She maintains a website at www.latoph.com.

Slavery…loyalty. Torture…honor. Betrayal…selflessness. All the young orphan wanted was security in a world that destroyed her family and left her despised and rejected. Can the simple farmgirl find a new family through voluntary enslavement to the duke's household? Crafted in a highly precise writing style so smooth it slips right from the page into your imagination, this fantastical storyworld examines timeless social issues that inform global justice today.

The Duke's Handmaid—ISBN: 978-09864517-3-7

Nor Iron Bars a Cage—ISBN: 978-09864517-6-8

Blood and Brine—ISBN: 978-1927154-20-5

p. a. baines

Paul writes science fiction that is both contemplative and profound. Educated in Africa, he works as an analyst/programmer and is studying towards a degree in Creative Writing through Buckinghamshire New University in England. He currently lives in a small corner of the Netherlands with his wife and two children and various wildlife.

Visit his website at www.pabaines.com. He is also a member of the New Authors' Fellowship.

From despair he fled, through tragedy he lived on, and journeyed to innocence.

His trajectory: the stars. His companion: a computer poised at the brink of sentience.

An unlikely friendship on a prototype spaceship at lightspeed towards Alpha Centauri, and redemption.

Alpha Redemption—ISBN: 978-09864517-4-4

Alpha Redemption was a finalist in the 2011 Next Generation Indie Book Awards, in the Science Fiction and Religious Fiction categories.

adam graham

Adam Graham is a mild-mannered goofball whose science fiction stories appear in *Residential Aliens, Light at the Edge of Darkness*, and in the *Laser & Sword* e-zine. His political column appears on Pajamasmedia.com and Renew America. He hosts the Truth and Hope Report podcast, the Old Time Dragnet Radio Show, the Great Detectives of Old Time Radio, and the Old Time Superman Radio Show. Mr. Graham holds a general studies Associate of Arts degree from Flathead Valley Community College with a concentration in Journalism.

His wife Andrea studied creative writing and religion at Ashland University, has been envisioning fantastic worlds since at least six, and has been writing science fiction novels since she was fourteen. She edited Adam's first novel, *Tales of the Dim Knight*, and is his editing partner for short stories too. She writes a regular devotion on her blog, http://christsglory.com, and writing advice and book reviews at http://povbootcamp.com.

Andrea and Adam live with their cat, Joybell, in Boise, Idaho.

What happens when the world's biggest superhero fan gets superpowers? When mild-mannered janitor Dave Johnson discovers an alien symbiote that gives him untold powers, there's only one thing to do: Put on a pair of tights and save the world. Follow Dave as he fights mobsters, aliens, and terrorists in a series of hilarious adventures, fighting crime and corruption while trying to keep his family together and avoid being sued for copyright infringement.

Tales of the Dim Knight—ISBN: 978-09864517-5-1

http://dimknight.com

r. L. copple

As a young teen, R. L. Copple played in his own make-believe world, writing the stories and drawing the art for his own comics while experiencing the worlds of other authors like Tolkien, Lewis, Asimov, and Lester Del Ray. After years of writing devotionally, he returned to the passion of his youth in order to combine his fantasy worlds and faith into the reality of the printed page.

Since then, his imagination has given birth to *The Reality Chronicles* trilogy, along with numerous short stories in various magazines. In his Texas Hill Country residence, he continues to create and give wings to new realities so that others might enjoy and be inspired by them. Visit his site at http://www.rlcopple.com.

Once upon a time, in a land far, far away, reality invaded the world. A mystical ring binds Sisko to bless others with miracles and avoid using its power for himself, which would lead to a curse. With his friends Josh the wizard and Seth the leader of a gang of thieves, Sisko explores the emerging reality through his travels and adventures. Journey with Sisko as reality's presence confronts and changes the greedy, the killers, the trapped, the demonic, and Sisko himself...Reality has dawned, and no one will be the same.

Reality's Dawn—ISBN: 978-0-9864517-7-5
Reality's Ascent—ISBN: 978-0-9864517-9-9
Reality's Fire—ISBN: 978-1-927154-24-3

travis perry

Travis Perry was born in Montana in 1968 and raised in that state. *The Crystal Portal*, published in 2011, was his first novel. He also contributed to the short story collections *Stories From a Soldiers Heart, Aquasynthesis, Aquasynthesis Again, Avenir Eclectia Volume 1, Colony Zero, No Revolution Too Big, Medieval Mars,* and *Avatars of Web Surfer*. As a publisher and owner of Bear Publications he has produced a number of short story collections, including most recently *Mythic Orbits 2016*. An Army Reserve officer who deployed for the Gulf War and later to Iraq, Afghanistan, and Africa, his writing reflects his lifelong interest in science fiction and fantasy, his strong Christian beliefs, and his knowledge of modern warfare..

mike Lynch

Mike Lynch is constantly awed by the wonder of God's creation, which has led to his interests in theology, astronomy, history, politics, and films, eventually turning his attention to writing. He published his first (non-fiction) book, *Dublin*, in 2007. His first novel, *When the Sky Fell*, co-authored by Brandon Barr, was published two years later, followed by two other books they've written together, *American Midnight* and *After the Cross*. *The Crystal Portal*, co-authored with Travis Perry, was released in 2011. Mike graduated from San Jose State with a degree in History, and from San Jose Bible College with a degree in Bible and Theology. He lives in the San Francisco Bay Area with his wife and two children.

Visit him online at http://www.mikelynchbooks.com.

For uncounted centuries the Deravans have sought unquestioned dominion over the galaxy, and they have found…us. Their armada of ships easily defeats Earth's defenses led by Commander Yamane, who has no choice but to seek the help of an enemy civilization he defeated in a war a decade before. The problem is, they have every reason not to come to Earth's rescue.

When the Sky Fell—ISBN: 978-0-9787782-3-1

(Silver Leaf Books)

An 800-year old letter unearthed at an archeological dig in Istanbul makes the astonishing claim the Cross of Jesus still exists, and has been safely hidden in Israel. A pair of archeologists race against time to locate this priceless treasure, but soon discover sinister forces are bent on stopping them at all costs.

After the Cross—ISBN: 978-0-9826242-0-3

(Ellechor Publishing)

keven newsome

Keven Newsome is a graduate student at the New Orleans Baptist Theological Seminary, where he is pursuing a Master of Arts in Theology specializing in Supernatural Theology. He writes stories that portray the supernatural and paranormal with a Biblical perspective. *Winter* is his first book. He currently lives in New Orleans, LA with his wife and their two children.

Keven also heads up the team at the New Authors' Fellowship collaborative blog: http://newauthors.wordpress.com. His website is at www.kevennewsome.com.

Winter Maessen didn't ask for the gift of prophecy. She's happy being a freak - but now everyone thinks she's crazy. Or evil.

Goths aren't all the same, you know. Some are Christians.
…Christians to whom God sends visions.

Students at her university are being attacked, and Winter knows there's more than flesh and blood at work.

Her gift means she's the only one who can stop it - but at what price?

Winter—ISBN: 978-9876531-0-9

kat heckenbach

Kat Heckenbach is a graduate of the University of Tampa, Magna Cum Laude, B.S. in Biology.

She spent several years teaching, but never in a traditional classroom–everything from Art to Algebra II—and now homeschools her two children.

Her writing spans the gamut from inspirational personal essays to dark and disturbing fantasy and horror, with over forty short fiction and nonfiction credits to her name. She is a member of the New Authors' Fellowship.

Enter her world at www.katheckenbach.com.

Angel doesn't remember her magical heritage…but it remembers her.

Magic and science collide when she embarks on a journey to her true home, and to herself.

Angel lives with a loving foster family, but dreams of a land that exists only in the pages of a fantasy novel. Until she meets Gregor, whose magic Talent saves her life and revives lost memories.

Angel follows Gregor to her homeland…a world unlike any she has imagined, where she travels a path of self-discovery that leads directly to her role in an ancient Prophecy…and to the madman who set her fate in motion.

Finding Angel—ISBN: 978-1-927154-01-4

ryan grabow

Ryan Grabow graduated from Long Island University in 2004, with a Bachelor's Degree in Electronic Media, and currently works in television production in Fort Myers, Florida. Caffeine is his first novel, combining his Christian faith with observations on how communications technology has impacted the reality of our lives, and drawing from his experience as a webmaster, programmer, and spiritual geek as points of speculation.

Ryan has a website at www.egrabow.com.

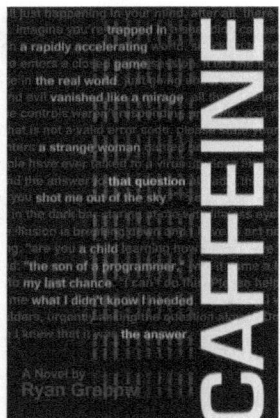

Brandon Dauphin feels like a dying ember. He's jobless and feels worthless, and falling in love has only made his problem worse. In an authoritarian and overstimulated 22nd-century America, all he can do to relieve his pain is indulge in the computer-simulated fantasies of a network called Dynamic Reality, until a virus takes control of the simulation. Unable to return to the real world, Brandon finds that the virus shares his questions about existence, and that she will stop at nothing for her answers.

Caffeine—ISBN: 978-1-927154-03-8

walt staples

According to Walt, the future trend of his life was probably foreshadowed when he was three. Riding with his parents, as they looked for a place to go to the bathroom on a Virginia fire trail, he was involved in a head-on collision with another family coming from the other direction also looking for a place to go to the bathroom. He credits this experience for his rather cockeyed view of the world.

Walt is a previous President of the Catholic Writers' Guild and contributes to their blog at http://blog.catholicwritersguild.com.

He is a top contributor to Splashdown's Avenir Eclectia microfiction project at http://www.avenireclectia.com and his short stories are widely published.

For a list of his works, visit http://gkfields.blogspot.com.

www.ingramcontent.com/pod-product-compliance
Lightning Source LLC
Chambersburg PA
CBHW020244150626
46552CB00020B/139